William Stamer

The Gentleman Emigrant

Vol. II

William Stamer

The Gentleman Emigrant
Vol. II

ISBN/EAN: 9783337188795

Printed in Europe, USA, Canada, Australia, Japan

Cover: Foto ©Andreas Hilbeck / pixelio.de

More available books at **www.hansebooks.com**

THE

GENTLEMAN EMIGRANT:

HIS DAILY LIFE, SPORTS, AND PASTIMES

IN

CANADA, AUSTRALIA, AND THE UNITED STATES.

By W. STAMER,

AUTHOR OF

"RECOLLECTIONS OF A LIFE OF ADVENTURE," ETC.

"UBI BENE IBI PATRIA."

IN TWO VOLUMES.

VOL. II.

LONDON:

TINSLEY BROTHERS, 8, CATHERINE STREET, STRAND.

1874.

LONDON:
SAVILL, EDWARDS AND CO., PRINTERS, CHANDOS STREET,
COVENT GARDEN.

CONTENTS

OF

THE SECOND VOLUME.

———

BACKWOODS FARM.

(*Continued.*)

THE present scarcity of pine timber is not so much owing to the amount that has been converted into lumber as to the destruction caused by fire. In Nova Scotia, as in New Brunswick, fire has been the ruin of the lumbering interest, and the amount of damage done by the devouring element is incalculable. A prairie on fire is a sublime sight, but the blaze is that of a farthing rushlight in comparison with one of these forest conflagrations. Perhaps the greatest fire on record is that which devastated the Miramichi woods in the year 1825. The summer of that year had been unusually dry; but although fires had broken out in different parts of the vast forest, stretching away northwards to the Canadian line, and westwards to the American boundary, little danger was apprehended by the inhabitants of the devoted district. The morning of the 7th of October broke with portentous calmness. Not a breath of wind was there to fan the smouldering fires, and a heavy cloud of black smoke hung like a vast pall over the forest. Warned by their unerring instincts, deer and other wild animals fled from their coverts, and sought refuge in the opens, an example which was unfortunately not followed by the unsuspecting settlers. Towards evening a gale suddenly sprang up from the westward, and before eight o'clock it was blowing a hurricane. All at once there was heard a roar as of distant artillery, a sheet of flame shot high into the air, clouds of blinding smoke came sweeping along before the fierce blast—the work of destruction had commenced. Too late to fly to the sea coast, all that the wretched inhabitants could do was to rush into the nearest lake or river. It would be difficult to imagine anything more truly appalling than the position of these unfortunates on that October night. Hemmed in on every side by walls of flame, burning wood and cinders falling in clouds around them, suffocated with smoke, and up to their necks in water—since the destruction of Pompeii never were mortals in sorer plight. Rarely, by all accounts, has the sun risen on a scene of greater desolation than that which the lately verdant forest presented on the morning of the 8th. Six thousand square miles of fire-swept country, a blackened, smoking, hideous expanse, with here and there a dismantled house or smouldering shanty.

Many perished in the flames, and more were burnt or injured by the falling timber. Few cattle escaped, and so intense was the heat that thousands of salmon and other fish were killed in the streams and rivers. The damage done to property was estimated at 228,000*l.*, and the value of the timber destroyed at 500,000*l.* ; and this one night's work!

Surrounded as he is by such highly inflammable matter, that the backwoodsman should be cautious in the use of matches would only be natural; but strange as it may seem, in his love for a bonfire he is a very child. The teamster trudging along the highway, the lumberman on the drive, the moose-caller out for his holiday, all have their pockets crammed with lucifer matches, which they use, regardless of consequences, whenever the whim seizes them. When they camp out they leave the fire to spread, fling the match with which they have lighted their pipe into the dry leaves and bushes, and not unfrequently set fire to the under brush just for the fun of the thing, or to have what they facetiously call a "torch." Nine-tenths of these backwoods fires owe their origin to the mischievous pranks or carelessness of lumbermen, and

until some law is passed by which offenders
shall be severely punished, fires must necessarily
be of constant recurrence. Let a fire in these pine
woods once get a good start, and there is no
telling when or where it will be extinguished.
It may be confined to a few hundred acres, it
may devastate six thousand square miles of
country, like the one at Miramichi.

Inexhaustible as seemed the supply of pine
timber in these woods some twenty years since,
the amount now available is only sufficient, according to competent judges, to keep the mills
going full time for ten or twelve years more.
Timber there is in abundance ; but so far from
lake or river, that the cost of hauling would be
more than its marketable value. What the millowners will do when the supply ceases they do
not very well know themselves. If the timber
would only grow up again on the burnt lands,
lumbering might, after the lapse of a score years
or so, be resumed with profit. But unfortunately
timber, or such timber at least as is required,
will not do so. No sooner does a fire sweep
over pine land than up starts a different
growth of timber. Fir, poplar, hackmatack take
the place of pine and spruce ; hemlock land is
overspread with cedar and alder, whilst maple,
beech, and birch are succeeded by spruce, sumach,

and raspberry and gooseberry bushes. The fire which spreads with such fearful rapidity through the resinous pine timber, makes but little impression on the hardwood land. In very dry seasons it occasionally runs through the underbrush, consuming here and there a dead oak or fallen maple ; but the green leaves smother the flame, and its onward course is soon arrested. Lucky it is for the lumbering interest that these pine forests are intersected at intervals by hardwood ridges, as, were it not for these fire-proof barriers, the first fire would sweep across the peninsula, from the Atlantic to the Bay of Fundy.

Cœlebs is now suffering from that very dangerous malady, logging on the brain. Mr. Seth Kempton, a smart gentleman who owns a few hundred acres of very indifferent timber land some five miles distant, has been endeavouring to persuade him that a hatful of dollars is to be made by lumbering, and that he, Cœlebs, could not do better than purchase the timber land in question. There need be no trouble about the purchase-money. Cœlebs can commence logging right away, and pay him when the logs are sold at the end of the season. Guesses that Mr. Cœlebs is just the right sort of man for the business, and will make a pile of dollars for sure. And poor Cœlebs is nibbling at the bait held out, and has been hard at work for some days making calculations as to the probable outlay and ultimate profits of the undertaking. That a profit there will be he is confident. The thing is as plain as the nose on one's face. To amount paid for land so many dollars. To so many men at so much per month, so many. To hauling logs, so many. To rafting and driving, so many. To provisions, so many. Deduct expenses from amount received for logs, and there remains, — dollars — cents clear profit (Q.E.D.)

Hoping that the disease might assume a mild form, and gradually effect its own cure, we have hitherto humoured the sick man by agreeing with him in everything; but this —— day of November, complications being imminent (the invalid has expressed his intention of closing with Kempton at once), we think the time has arrived to administer a mild emetic, the said emetic being our own logging experiences. The opportunity is soon afforded us. The post-prandial-pipe lighted, Master Cœlebs produces his logging calculations, and goes hammer and tongs at his interminable additions and subtractions. To land so much—to men so much, &c. &c. Subtract from value of logs, &c. Balance profit, — dollars — cents.

"That's correct, is it not?"

"No !"

" No ? What can we know about it ?"

" Just as much as it is possible for any man to learn in two seasons."

" What ! We have had a turn at logging— why didn't we tell him so before ?"

" Because we didn't think it would interest him to know it."

" Interest him ! Of course it does. How did we. pull it off ?"

" On the first occasion we were eight hundred dollars out of pocket; on the second we managed to clear about the same amount."

" How did we manage to lose ?"

" By going it alone."

" And to gain ?"

" By going shares with an experienced lumberman, who did the bossing and kept the men to their work, whilst we acted as commissary."

" But we must have gone very stupidly to work to lose in the first instance ?"

" Of course we did, just as stupidly as any man might be expected to do who undertook a business of which he knew nothing.

" It was shortly after our introduction to backwoods life, and when we were still as green as any hemlock, that we made our first essay in lumbering. Healthful and pleasant occupation

during the winter months being our object, and
profit a secondary consideration, our operations
were conducted on a very limited scale, our crew
consisting of five axemen, a cook, and a teamster.
We did the bossing, and if ever boss was disposed
to treat his men kindly we were that boss.   The
idea of passing the winter in the woods having
only entered our head at the time when others
had already commenced chopping, we were rather
later in the field than was altogether desirable.
By the time camp and barn were built, hay and
meal for the horses and oxen, and provisions for
the men, hauled out, it was the 1st of December.
On the 2nd the men arrived; on the 3rd the first
tree was 'fallen.'   For a fortnight or so everything went along smoothly.   To an inexperienced
woodsman like ourself the number of trees felled
daily sounded highly satisfactory.   Mr. Teamster
appeared to be hard at work with his oxen from
daylight till dusk, when Mr. Cook was not
making bread or flap-jacks or fish-balls he was
fiddling.   The life being a novel one, we enjoyed
ourselves hugely.   An hour before daybreak we
would turn out of our bunk and help the cook
with the breakfast, which we shared with the
men, as likewise dinner and supper; for although
the cook's cooking was on a par with his fiddling, of the vilest, we thought it wiser to put

up with it than by eating apart, to raise the
republican dander of our crew. Our self-denial
was not very grievous, for we had arrived at that
state of health when dough-boys are almost as
easily digested as lead, flap-jacks as sheet iron.
Breakfast over, we would accompany the men to
their work, and amuse ourselves with lopping, or
else engage in a little amateur hauling with our
ponies. During the daytime we had plenty of
employment. In the evening we would smoke
our Virginny by the blazing camp fire, and listen
to the songs and stories of the men and to the
squeaking of the cook's fiddle. In a word, we
led a lumberman's life, and enjoyed it. At the
end of a fortnight, meal or something else being
wanted, we put the ponies to the sled, and telling
the men that we should not be back for a day or
two, and to work well during our absence, we
started for the settlements. On our way out we
stopped at a camp where we knew the crew to
be the same strength as our own, to compare
notes with the boss lumberman, a French Canadian, with whom we had hunted the preceding
Fall. He was ravished to see us. How did it go?"

"First-rate; and with him?"

"Like that. He had only so many logs cut
and so many hauled, andwas just a little behind-
hand."

"The start we gave did not escape the quick eye of Monsieur Jean Baptiste."

"What! Hadn't we done as well as that?"

"Not quite. We had just cut and hauled one-half that number, and our logs were considerably smaller than his."

"But, *Sapristi!* our men must have been famously amusing themselves. Only one way to arrange oneself with those gentry there—to put them to the door if they work not."

"And after?"

"Engage others."

"And if they are not to be had?"

"Ah, then——"

"We did not say much, but we thought a good deal, and instead of absenting ourselves for a couple of days, as had been our intention, the instant we got our supplies we turned the ponies' heads woodwards. It was too late to reach the shanty the same night, but we arrived there two hours after daybreak the next morning, and, on pushing open the door, beheld axemen, teamster, and cook quietly warming their shins at the fire. And why were they not at work?"

"Oh, they had overslept themselves."

"Had they, indeed. And it was for that reason possibly that they were endeavouring to make up for lost time by having an after-breakfast chat by the fire."

" Well, there was no use getting riled about it. They had worked hard since they came, and the loss of a couple of hours didn't much signify.

" We had determined to make no mention of our interview with Jean Baptiste, but for the future to work less and watch more; but this barefaced assertion of the teamster so incensed us that we let drive.

" Work well! What did they call working well? In the same space of time the Frenchman's crew down at Big Clear had done more than double the work, and they were far from being a smart crowd. Hitherto we had said nothing, but for the future we should insist upon their performing a fair day's work, and, if they could not or would not, they might go.

" From that hour every man Jack of them became possessed with the demon of sulkiness. No more singing and story-telling, no more jokes and laughter; the cook hung up his fiddle and his bow-o-oh! and our shanty of harmony became a veritable shanty of discord. Little improvement was apparent in the work done. We kept a sharp eye on the men, but it availed nothing. To watch them swinging their axes one would imagine that they *were* doing their 'level' best, but the trees felled were not in proportion to the blows struck. When to 'put in the time' is the lumberman's resolve all the

watching in the world wont prevent him. He
can deliver the strokes of his axe in such a way
that half the effect is lost, and by cutting the
notch a little to one side or a little to the other,
fall the tree so as to lodge it in the branches of
another, and thus protract the work ; or his axe
is notched, and he must go grind it; or he has
cut himself, and must go fetch a piece of rag.
Plausible excuses are never wanting for absenting
himself for from ten minutes to an hour at a
time.   It is the same with your teamster.   He
must lay down a piece of corduroy, here cut a
new road, or there a *Buck* is sick or *Bright*, or the
bob-sled is broken, and he must go get it mended.
The cook takes it out of you in wastefulness.
The way in which he makes flour and pork vanish
is a caution, and should you venture to observe
that the provisions are going rather fast, he will
ask you, with an air of injured innocence, if it is
your intention to starve your crew, if so you had
better tell him. The long and short of the matter
is that they prefer working for one of their own
stamp and a fellow-townsman than for a gentleman and a stranger.   Tom This and Bill That
lumber because lumbering is their business.
Mr. Cœlebs and Mr. Benedict lumber because
they think themselves uncommon smart, and the
sooner that idea is taken out of them the better.
What is the good of strangers coming if no more

is to be made out of them than out of old Uncle
Ford, who has been in the woods since he was
the height of an axe-helve? Hang strangers!'

" If we have heard that argument once we have
heard it a score of times, and it is one reason
why we have so little faith in the gentleman lumberer. But there are others equally weighty.
To lumber, with any chance of success, one must
have been brought up to the business. No one
but a thorough backwoodsman can calculate even
approximately the value of timber land. That
there are good trees in the lot amounts to nothing.
Better small logs and plenty of water to drive
them than big ones when the water is distant or
of insufficient depth. An extra mile or so of
hauling swallows up the profits, having to employ double crews, for driving and damming
brings the lumberman into debt. Not only is
experience requisite in the purchase of timber
land, but in the sale of the logs. Millowners are
keenly alive to their own interests, and when
dealing with a green hand their measurement of
logs is by rule of thumb. The verb to cheat
having been expunged from American dictiona-
ries as low and old-countryfied, they do not cheat
Mr. Greenhorn, but they do a remarkably smart
trade with him—get ten or fifteen per cent. the
advantage of him in the measurement of his logs,
and the same in the store accounts if they furnish

him with supplies on credit. If he thinks the
measurement is not correct he had better go
measure them himself—a thing much more easily
said than done. Again, to attempt to combine
farming with lumbering is, in most cases, a losing
game; one pursuit is pretty certain to be carried
on at the expense of the other. During the
winter months the backwoods farmer can find
profitable employment for men and oxen in the
green woods, but by logging for others at so
much a week or month, not on his own account.
River-driving and rafting clash with spring
ploughings and sowings—it is crops or logs, and
the settler has to choose between them. Logging
cannot be prosecuted by fits and starts. It is
not by lumbering one season and farming the
next that men make money, but by keeping at it
right along—setting off one year's gains against
another year's losses. It is a very risky business, and the lumberer is even more dependent
on the seasons than the farmer. Should the
winter be an open one the hauling is bad, and he
has difficulty in getting his logs to the water;
and if the spring prove dry he may not be able
to drive them. He must wait until the Fall
rains, or until the following spring, and if he
cannot afford to wait he must sell them as they
'jam' to some millowner or boss lumberman,

who will take them 'at a fair valuation,' *i.e.*, at
a price which will not cover the poor logger's
working expenses. We were so far fortunate
that winter and spring proved alike favourable ;
had they not done so, our losses would have been
proportionately greater. We lost eight hundred
dollars, and gained fully that amount of experience—experience which enables us to tell you,
friend Cœlebs, that if you commence logging on
your own account you will repent it. Under the
most favourable circumstances you may possibly
cover expenses ; more than that you need not
expect. If to log you are determined, go shares
with a native, and whilst he looks after the men
do you attend to the commissariat. In that way,
and in no other, you may contrive to make a few
hundred dollars each season. But that you may
not be done you will have to keep a sharp eye on
your partner. Every agreement made should be
in black and white, every bill paid receipted,
every log hauled entered into your own private
note-book, and when the raft is sold it is indispensable that you have a duly-qualified measurer
and valuer to look after your interests, a stranger
to the place if possible, as 'townies' are apt to
play into each other's hands."

Christmas has come round again, and we are
going to keep it in good old English style. The

house, now partially furnished, has been profusely
decorated with evergreens, the mincemeat has
been made, the pudding mixed, the " lordly"
turkey sacrificed. For Christmas merry-makings
there are many worse places than the backwoods—
the Australian bush, for example. When the
thermometer stands at 90° or 100° in the shade,
the very sight of roast-beef and plum-pudding
creates nausea, and the wassail-bowl must be iced,
not spiced, to be grateful. Father Christmas is
not at home in the Sunny South. His domain is
the frozen North, where lie the snow and the ice,
and the hoar frost, and where shall they be
found if not in the New Dominion? Dinner
over, and the exile's toast, "Here's to the dear
old land, and all true friends across the water,"
having been drunk with enthusiasm, we draw
our chairs to the fire and speak of bygone Christ-
mases ; and as poor Cœlebs recalls the many
happy ones he has passed at the old home in
——shire, his voice grows somewhat husky, and
a tear glistens on the eyelash. But when our
time comes, and we proceed to tell of certain
dismal ones spent by us in foreign parts—more
particularly of one terrible Christmas-day when
we were lost in the Australian bush, and were
nearly succumbing from heat and want of water,
he brightens up considerably, and on wishing us

good night, says cheerfully, "After all, old fellow, there are many worse places than the backwoods."

Yes; there are many worse places than the backwoods—the backwoods proper, not the clearings. Where would a man of Cœlebs's limited means be able to live as comfortably and as independently? With an outlay of a few hundred pounds, and a yearly income of from fifty to a hundred, he need want for nothing, not even for society. For six months out of the twelve, or for one-half of the fishing season, and the whole of the hunting, there are plenty of agreeable men in Halifax and elsewhere who would be only too happy to accept his hospitality; and the exercise of that hospitality need cost him nothing, or next to nothing, for the backwoods visitor is expected to bring his own luxuries with him, and the necessaries of life are cheap. Drawbacks there are, and great ones, the greatest, in our opinion, being the yearly plague of flies. To say that during the months of May and June the flies are excessively troublesome in the woods is a very mild way of putting it. They are perfectly unendurable, making the backwoodsman's life a burden to him, and unless he have the hide of a rhinoceros, all he can do is to shut himself up in the house until such time as they may be pleased to take their departure. In Canada and the United States the second spring, or Indian summer, goes far to compensate one for the loss of the first. But when, as in Nova Scotia, there is little or no Indian summer, it comes hard. To lose two months—the very months of all others when nature is freshest and greenest, and when, after the long hibernation, one longs to bask in the sunshine and thaw one-self out—is enough to make an angel swear, let alone a "human." Another drawback is the plague of helps. It is next to impossible to keep a decent servant. American helps are sociably inclined. They like to go to meeting on Sunday, and have a quiet "gas" with the folk at store and market, and in the woods there is neither meeting-house nor forum. The most considerate of treatment and the highest of wages will not tempt them to remain with you. After a month or six weeks they feel home-sick, give notice, bundle, and go. Cœlebs has been fortunate in securing the services of Mr. and Mrs. Mac, but he pays them very high wages, and lets them do pretty much as they please. It would never answer to have such people on a large farm, for Mac, although a very handy fellow, is not equal to a hard day's work, and his wife is neither strong enough nor smart enough for the dairy.

Then there is the disadvantage of being a long way from town, not on account of the difficulty in obtaining supplies, but in respect to letters and papers. It is not always that a man can be found willing to carry the mail, and when he is found, less than two dollars it is useless to offer him. Twenty miles through the woods is equal to thirty along the high road—twice thirty are sixty—a good two days' tramp, and a dollar a day is bare wages. Two dollars a week are one hundred and four dollars, or twenty-one pounds sterling per annum, and that is altogether too much for postage. Such annoyances as an invitation to appear before Solon Quirk, Esquire, Justice of the Peace, &c., and the apparition from time to time of a crew of boorish lumbermen, need not enter into the calculation, for summonses are easily avoided; and when lumbermen find that their presence is not desired, they soon cease to honour one with their agreeable society.

It is not the young unmarried man, fond of fishing and shooting and hard as nails, that would be likely to find backwoods life intolerable, but the delicate married woman with a young family. We know that in her eyes all the advantages of cheap living, pure air, freedom, and independence are apt to seem more than counterbalanced by the dreadful fact that she lives miles away from a doctor, and that in the event of sickness an entire day may elapse before Mr. Squills can be at the bedside of the sufferer. The very thought of what might happen if any of the children were to be taken suddenly ill makes her shudder, and Tommy cannot cough nor Kitty look flushed without her feeling convinced that it is the commencement of croup or scarlatina. Not only does she feel the loss of the doctor, but of the parson. It is dreadful to live in a place where the church-going bell is never heard, where there is neither chapel nor meeting-house, and where one day is so precisely similar to another that unless one take good note of time it is impossible to distinguish Sunday from week-day. And then no schools to which to send the children, their only instruction such as father and mother can give them. To think of one's sons growing up like young Indians, experter with the paddle than with the pen, better trappers than arithmeticians, and one's daughters like squaws, their only accomplishments basket-making and bead-work. It is shocking.' She would have been a hundred thousand times happier in the most miserable back settlement.

So she thinks—but would she? It is our

humble opinion that she would not. Back settlement life, as Cœlebs justly says, is backwoods life without its freedom and its pleasures. The advantages of back townships exist only in the imagination; when weighed in the balance of common sense they amount to nothing. The back township settler has a doctor. So he has, and more to be pitied he. There are no doubt honourable exceptions, but taking them as a body, back settlement practitioners are not the most brilliant of men. When they hear a man's teeth chattering like a hundred pair of castanets, they guess he has fever and ague, and they administer quinine, and when the patient complains of pain in his heart (the backwoodsman's heart, like Paddy's, lies in the region of his stomach) and of feeling "real sick," they guess he has eaten too much fat pork and fixins, and give him a blue pill. They can attend a midwifery case, set a broken bone, and bind up an axe-cut; beyond that their professional aid and advice is seldom worth having. When the ailment is not of the ordinary backwoods type, their diagnosis is mere guesswork. They make a shot, overhaul their pharmacopœia for the treatment to be pursued in such a case, and if that has not the desired effect, guess again and take a new departure. But they are often worse

than ignorant; they are rash. They will pre-
scribe in cases which they well know are too
intricate for them, and undertake to perform
operations that many an able surgeon would
decline. We know one young backwoods, Bob
Sawyer, who prescribed for and killed a poor
fellow suffering from cancer, and another of the
same stamp who attempted the operation for
cataract, and put his patient's eye out. It is
better to have no doctor than a bad one; and as
in back townships good ones are the exception,
nothing would be gained, so far as medical
assistance was concerned, by living there. Every
man whose home is in the woods should have
some slight knowledge of surgery. He should
be able at least to bandage up a wound and to
apply a tourniquet, and he should be provided
with a small medicine-chest and the *Family
Medical Reference*. Backwoods ailments are
seldom very complicated—they generally yield
to simple remedies, and it is only when the
doctor steps in, and begins prescribing his
powders, draughts, and bolus that the sufferer is
in any real danger.

As regards the second disadvantage, the
absence of any place of worship, we shall only
observe that it is not invariably those whose
houses lie nearest the Church who are the

nearest to heaven, and that the Omnipotent can be as reverently worshipped in the leafy aisles of the primeval forest as in the most gorgeous of Christian temples.

Whether the absence of a school is a disadvantage, depends on the social status of the parents. National schools, such as one finds in the back townships of Canada and the United States, are in every way adapted to the requirements of the ordinary run of settlers, but they are not precisely the kind of academies to which a gentleman would like to send his children. It is doubtless very amusing to read of the rough-and-ready way in which instruction is imparted by the American skulemarm, but not so amusing to know that one's own child is being thus instructed, and that his class-mates are little ragamuffins whose parents hail from the wilds of Connemara. The man who had any real regard for his children would much prefer to instruct them himself, and he could do that in the woods. The only accomplishments that girls would be likely to acquire in a back settlement would be singing, or the nasal harmony which passes muster for it, quilting, and patchwork; and if they were very smart indeed, they might possibly attain to cross-stitch, and achieve a kettle-holder or a marker for the family Bible. In the larger towns there are excellent schools where boys are prepared for the learned professions, and where girls are taught everything, from sewing on a button to bravura singing and water-colour drawing. But hamlets are not towns, and in back settlements educational advantages in a liberal sense there are none. The only advantages that we can discover which the clearings possess over the backwoods are that in the clearings there is comparative immunity from the plague of flies, and that the plague of helps is less baneful. But tastes differ. Some women take as naturally to the woods as ducks to the water, whilst others are quite out of their element, and are as miserable as miserable can be. Everything depends on a woman's temperament, more especially upon her adaptability. Education and social position have little to do with it; but as a rule, the more refined the woman, the greater the chance of her being able to adapt herself to backwoods life. To the vulgar, ignorant woman nothing is more dreadful than solitude. Having no resources in herself without society of some description, her existence is a blank, and she would prefer to live in the most wretched back settlement, and have neighbours with whom to gossip, than in a terrestrial paradise with no other companion than her husband. The well-bred woman, on the contrary, is not entirely dependent on others for her entertainment. She likes society, but not the society which back townships afford. She has no ambition to be queen of her company, and would rather have the society of her husband than that of a legion of settlers' wives, no matter how sociably inclined. She is his constant companion, and, to a great extent, whatever amuses and interests him is amusing and interesting to her likewise. In the winter she sleighs with him, and skates with him, and toboggings with him, and accompanies him in his rambles through the snow-decked forest. In the spring she helps him to make maple-sugar, to garden, and to catch trout, and when the black flies arrive, and all outdoor work and amusements are for a time suspended, she is his comforter in affliction; and should he rashly determine, black flies or no black flies, to catch a dish of fish, she, like a good Venus, prepares him for battle by enveloping his head in the ample folds of her own veil, and by sewing up all dangerous rents and apertures, and when he returns bleeding from the fray, anoints his wounds with oil and camphor. In summer she is his boat-boy. She minds the jib-sheet, steers when required, or takes hold of an oar or a paddle on an emergency. When pic-nicing or camping out, she is the squaw who

minds the wigwam. Whilst her lord catches
fish and cleans them (fish-cleaning is not amongst
her duties) she collects hemlock boughs for the
bed, and sticks and birch bark for the fire, boils
the water, and beats up the batter for the pancakes; and should it come to roughing, it is not
from her lips that proceeds the grumbling. When
an ordinary woman would cry and wring her
hands, she bursts into a merry peal of laughter.
She contrasts the rude log shanty in which they
have taken shelter with the well-remembered
drawing-room at home; the empty flour barrel on
which she has laid the tin platters and pannikins,
with some well-appointed dinner table; her high,
hob-nailed boots and lindsey petticoat with the
elegant toilets of days gone by, and is not in
the least discontented. *Les extrêmes se touchent.*
In the great world it would be dreadful to do
one's own cooking, to drink out of tin pannikins,
to use one's fingers for forks, to dine off fried fish
and pancakes, to sleep without sheets, and to
have no new dresses. But in the woods—ah!
that is quite another thing. In the woods as in
the woods, and the nearer the approach to savage
life the greater the enjoyment.

In the summer she goes huckleberrying, and
cranberrying, is her husband's gilly on his shooting
excursions, and when trapping begins, she enters

into the business with all the keenness of an Indian
or half-bred. Fur is her perquisite. It is the only
luxury after which she hankers. Silks and
velvets are out of place in the woods, but fur is
never out of place where the thermometer descends
below zero.

But it is not all play. Sleighing and skating
and boating and camping out are her amusements,
and she has her fair share of work. How does
she adapt herself to that? Just as readily as to
those sports and pastimes which in England
would be considered tom-boyish. She has a
regular routine laid down for herself, and by
following it, her duties, though manifold, are
never burdensome. Every morning, immediately
after breakfast, she repairs to the kitchen, and
whilst Biddy or Ayeshah makes the beds, prepares with her own fair fingers such pies and
" chicken-fixins " as are beyond her handmaidens'
culinary skill. Beds made, and pies and cakes
ready for the oven, she starts on her grand rounds,
visits the larder, the dairy, the poultry-yard, and
lastly, the shanty, where she has her daily
conference with her Mrs. Mac about cows,
calves, pigs, poultry, cream, butter, eggs, and
farm produce generally. If it is washing-day,
she helps her help in the laundry. But in
well-organized American households, washing-

day has no terrors; it is a "heavy wash" that cannot be got through in two hours. There is no messing and slopping and soaping, and rubbing as in an English farmhouse. With one of Doty's patent washing machines and wringers, the linen is washed and wrung without the operator so much as wetting her fingers. It is only the ironing that is tedious, but in the woods a little ironing goes a very long way. Unless she have children to look after, her morning's work is over by twelve o'clock, and from that hour until dinner her time is at her own disposal. After dinner she gets her work-basket, and whilst her husband reads to her the "Latest Intelligence," she sews, and knits and darns like a good housewife—in winter by the cheerful hardwood fire, in summer on the verandah.

Such briefly told is the daily life of the backwoodswoman who has the precious bump of adaptability. The character is not ideal, but drawn from life.

The life of the backwoodswoman who has not that bump may be summed up in one word— dumps. To her spring, summer, autumn, and winter are synonymous with the season of flies, the season of heats, the season of rains, and the season of snows—one worse than the other. In her prosaic mind the soft greens of spring and summer, the gorgeous hues of autumn, the dazzling whites of winter, mean simply that the trees are in full leaf, that the leaves are decaying, that there has been a fall of snow. Like the American young lady whose admiration of Niagara was centred in the rainbow above the Falls, because it so reminded her of a certain "love of a bonnet"—Nature's colouring is associated in her mind with that of the dyer. Green becomes her to perfection, the purples and scarlets and yellows of the autumnal woods would be sweetly pretty could they only be woven into a Cashmere. Skating and tobogging and boating, and such rough outdoor amusements are not to her taste. She is no hoiden or white squaw. As to cooking and dairying and washing it would be barbarous to ask her to attempt such menial work. She has had the education of a lady, and knows as much of housekeeping as David Copperfield's child-wife. The poor woman is never happy except when she is miserable, or when she goes on a visit to some friend in the settlements, for of course she has her outing occasionally. It must not be supposed that because a lady lives in the backwoods that she is tied there hand and foot. In Australia, owing to the enormous distances, the up-country squatter's wife is, to a great extent, a fixture on the station, but with the backwoods settler's wife it is very different. Cœlebs lives in the heart of the backwoods—much further from a settlement than most men would care to live, but he is by the direct road only eighteen miles from L——, a town of five thousand inhabitants. The road, if none of the best, is practicable during the winter months in sled, and on horseback at all seasons. Supposing that he kept a pony for his wife, she could, by starting at eight o'clock, be in L—— by midday, and, unless very timid, she would have no need of an escort. From man she would have nothing to fear, and as little from beast or reptile. We have said a good deal, perhaps more than was altogether necessary, of the bad points of the lumberman and the backwoodsman ; let us here record a good one. In his own peculiar way he is extremely courteous or rather respectful to women. He does not take off his hat and salaam and make pretty speeches, but his services are ever at their disposal—he will run, fetch, and carry for them, and would bite his tongue off sooner than say anything that would be likely to offend. If a storm came on, or night should overtake a lady in the woods, she might seek the shelter of a lumberman's camp without inquietude. Not a word would be uttered in her presence at which umbrage could be taken—

every man of the crew would do his utmost to make her comfortable; and if she stood in need of a guide or escort, however busy they might be, a hand would be spared to accompany her. Backwoodsmen are, as a rule, exceedingly hospitable, and so likewise are the settlers and the townsfolk. Unless Mrs. Cœlebs thinks proper to give herself airs she will not want for invitations. Not only will the good people of L—— be ready to receive her, but they will feel extremely hurt should she decline their hospitality, and the oftener she avails herself of it the better pleased they will be. If to attend church regularly every Sunday be indispensable to her happiness and peace of mind, it is not the dread of hotel bills that need prevent her. She can ride out to L—— every Saturday afternoon, spend Saturday and Sunday nights with her friends, and return home on Monday morning. During the fly season— which is also the bathing season—she can likewise accept their hospitality, and in the fall of the year, when the woods are at their best, she can return the compliment by inviting them to visit her in their turn.

To compare the clearings with the backwoods : In the clearings one cannot, without giving mortal offence, select one's company—in the woods one can. In the clearings it is next to

impossible to amuse a visitor—in the woods
nothing is more easy. In the clearings one's
every movement is watched and criticised by
prying and gossiping neighbours—in the woods
one is almost as free as air. In the clearings the
well-bred man and woman will not find a single
advantage which cannot equally be found in the
backwoods—but in the backwoods they will enjoy
many advantages which cannot be enjoyed in the
clearings. That is our opinion, and it is the
opinion of many well-bred, well-educated men
and women of our acquaintance. If one cannot
live in the woods one can at least vegetate
luxuriantly. In the clearings one can neither live
nor vegetate. The man who has the means to
purchase a farm in a long settled district would
be a fool to locate himself in the woods ; but when
the choice lies between the clearings and by the
clearings—we mean all new townships and
sparsely populated districts—and the woods, the
latter is certainly the more preferable of the two.
But we would not advise any man to go to work
in the same way as friend Cœlebs. Until he had
given the life a fair trial, and felt convinced that
it suited him, he should not expend on improvements one cent more than was absolutely necessary. One can always build, but one cannot
always sell. A log house is not as fine as a

frame one, but it is just as warm and snug, and the cost of erection is trifling. Such a log house and barn as he would require ought not to cost more than fifty pounds, and, if the life proved distasteful, that is all he would be out of pocket, for if the land was worth anything it should be worth what he gave for it, and if he could not find an immediate purchaser he could wait. But he should give the life a fair trial—two years at the very least. To the man fresh from the busy world the backwoods seem very lonely, but this feeling of loneliness gradually wears away. Were we in Cœlebs's position, young, strong, healthy, and with a capital limited to one or two thousand pounds, we should do as he has done—make us a home in the wilderness, not in the maritime provinces, but in Upper or Lower Canada. We could never adapt ourselves to clearing life, but we could to that of the backwoods. We do not merely think so; we are certain of it, for we have made the experiment. That we should have an occasional touch of the blues is likely enough. It would be impossible to altogether banish from one's mind the pomps and vanities of this wicked world—the many charms of advanced civilization; but when we felt the attack coming on we should endeavour

to overcome it by a little common-sense reasoning. We would picture to ourselves all the
delights of London and Paris, all the picked
spots of Europe—the vine-clad hills of Rhineland, the lakes, rivers, and snow-capped peaks of
Switzerland and Tyrol, the smiling shores of
Como and Maggiore—Venice, Florence, Rome,
Naples—and then quietly ask ourselves the
question : " On your miserable pittance what kind
of a figure would you cut in these centres of
fashion ? What would be your life ? what your
amusements ? Without trade, profession, or
calling by which to eke it out, what could you
do on one hundred pounds per annum ?" In
London, oh, grumbler ! you would be obliged to
live in a back street, a very back street, for house-
rent ought not to exceed a sixth of one's income.
The sixth of a hundred is seventeen, and it is a
poor lodging that lets for 17$l.$ per annum. Your
food would be on a par with your lodging, of the
cheapest and of the plainest. The expenses of
the victualling department should not exceed
two-fifths of one's income. Two-fifths of a hundred is forty ; 40$l.$ per annum is but 2$s.$ 2$d.$ per
diem, and at the present price of meat and other
necessaries it is not much that can be bought for
that sum. One-fifth—20$l.$ for clothing ; rent,
17$l.$; food, 40$l.$; clothing, 20$l.$=77$l.$ There would

be only 23*l.* remaining for washing, firing, gas, taxes, &c., and amusements. Amusements! You might safely put a big zero after that item. It would be the same in Paris, in Vienna, in Florence, in any other great city. To enjoy city life you must have money, and you have none. Without money the gayest city would seem dull, the loveliest scene lose half its attraction. Wherever you went a phantom purse of consumptive aspect would be constantly before you, and a voice be ever whispering in your ear, "Only twenty-five pounds a quarter!" You would feel inclined for a cup of coffee and a cigar, and would be just on the point of entering some café when the dreadful vision would flit before you, and you would hear the words, "Beware, rash mortal! Only twenty-five pounds a quarter!" You would halt in front of a theatre and read the programme of the evening's performance. A new play! You would like to see it. You will purchase a ticket, but on the threshold of the ticket-office the phantom awaits you, and again you hear the warning words, "Remember! Only twenty-five pounds a quarter!" So long as you were exposed to temptation that spectral monitor would be always at your elbow, and would only leave you at the door of your apartment on the first-floor—down the chimney.

There would be no temptation there, unless it were to throw yourself out of the window.

Are you discontented because here in the wild woods are no cafés, no restaurants, no shops, no theatres? You ought rather to be thankful that at every step you are not called upon to resist temptation. Have you grown tired of the view from your window? Have forest, lake, and river lost their charm, the charm of novelty, and do you wonder what you could ever have seen in them to admire? Do you long for the sea, the mountains, the soft zephyrs and fragrant orange groves of the Sunny South? and do you feel perfectly convinced that you would never weary of Alpine scenery, or of gazing on the blue Tyrrhenean sea? Think what the old monk said of one of the fairest views on earth, that from the Convent of San Martino, at Naples: "Yes. It is fine, *transiuntibus!*" The old fellow had grown weary of looking down on the busy city beneath, of the bay, of Vesuvius, of the islands, just as men weary of everything in this world, just as you would grow weary of the most lovely prospect if you had nothing else to do than to look at it. Fine scenery may be likened to a zero; by itself it counts for nothing. You cannot eat it, nor drink it, nor clothe yourself with it. It is only when it comes after an unit that it has a

value. Money is that unit, and you have it not.
By reasoning in this way we should be able, we
think, to rout the blue devils and to convince
ourselves that, if not the luckiest and happiest
of mortals, we were far from being the most
wretched; that if for the rich man there are
many more desirable residences than the Canadian
backwoods, for the poor man there are many
worse.

We have completed our backwoods year; it is
the morning of our departure. From the verandah
we take a last look at the rushing river and at
lake and forest, now dazzlingly white in their
winter dress. It is with dimmed eyes that we
do so, for with all their disadvantages we love
the grand old woods. Shall we ever visit them
again? Who can tell? Five times have we said,
"Good night;" five times, "Good morrow."
"On revient toujours à ses premières amours,"
and one of our very earliest was "Sylva Ameri-
cana."

WE never hear an American boasting of his country's greatness without thinking of the Irishman at the Falls of Niagara.

" There!" cried Jonathan to newly arrived Paddy, as he waved his hand in the direction of the Horse-shoe Fall. "There! Now isn't that wonderful?" "Wontherful?" replied Pat. "What's wontherful?"

" Why, to see all that water come thundering over them rocks." "Faix, then, to tell ye the honest thruth," was the response, " I can't see anything very wontherful in that. Why, what the divil is there to hinther it from coming over?"

The United States is undoubtedly a great country, but what is there to hinder her greatness? Considering her advantages, it would be much more surprising if she were not great. With three million square miles of the finest land in the world, with hundreds of thousands of emigrants landing yearly on her shores, bringing with them skilled hands and millions upon

millions of dollars, with the experience of ages
to guide her, wealth and greatness came as a
matter of course; there is nothing wonderful in it.

Our experience of America and the Americans extends over a period of eighteen years.
Five different visits, varying in duration from
two months to twelve, have we paid the
Great Republic, and on each succeeding one
have we found occasion to modify or alter our
opinion of men and things. What have been
our experiences? When we think how easily
some men gain their information, we are
ashamed to own how very little it is that we
know. A two months' scamper across the
continent is sufficient, it would seem, to enable
a man to speak and write authoritatively of
American institutions. After three years' familiar intercourse with men of all classes of society,
we are obliged to confess that we have much
more to learn than we have learnt.

When first we travelled through the United
States, it was *en touriste,* and we were delighted
with everything, for everything was new, and
novelty is pleasing. Never were such hotels as
the American hotels, no such railway carriages
and steamers as American railway cars and
steamers, not an European watering-place half so
pleasant as Saratoga. Nothing we should like

more than to reside permanently in the United
States. The country was a splendid country,
and the people were trumps. We had a very
agreeable cicerone—no man more companionable
than the liberally educated American—and he
was always ready to improve the occasion. Was
finance the topic of conversation? Could anything possibly be more satisfactory than the
finances of the United States? Taxation merely
nominal, and always a handsome balance in the
treasurer's hands. How he did pity us, with
our crushing National Debt, and our budget of
sixty millions.

Was liberty the theme? That the United
States was the freest country in the world, there
could be no question whatever. Every citizen
of the age of twenty-one years had a voice in the
government of the country. He had a vote,
and that vote was hampered with no restrictions.
Bribery and corruption were unknown, intimidation was a thing unheard of. At the elections
every man voted as he thought fit, and no man
was there so humble that he might not aspire to
the Chief Magistracy. So long as a man obeyed
the laws, no one interfered with him. He was
at liberty to think as he liked, say what he
liked, live how he liked, whether troglodyte or

stylite was a matter of perfect indifference to the Sovereign People.

Seen through our friend's tinted American spectacles, every object assumed a roseate hue, and we returned home very favourably impressed with the country and the people.

On our second visit to the United States we travelled alone, and there being no longer the charm of novelty, we viewed things with a much more critical eye. The country was the same great country as ever, but the Sovereign People no longer came up to their former standard of perfection. It was at the time of the *know-nothing* movement, and foreigners were at a decided discount. The cry was, " Curse the Irish! to h—l with the Dutch; Americans to govern America! Hooray !" To own up to being an Englishman, with English proclivities, was to subject oneself to insult. England was the poorest, meanest, most contemptible country on the face of the globe, and Englishmen a cowardly, presumptuous, despicable lot, out of whom it was the mission of the Sovereign People to take the shine. When we say the Sovereign People, it must be borne in mind that it is of " King Mob" we are speaking—King Mob, whose presence is so painfully conspicuous at

every general election. In writing of a people,
precedence must be given to the governing
classes, and in the United States, New York
more especially, the mob rules.

On our second visit to the Great Republic we
made the acquaintance of the Sovereign People,
and the more we saw of them the less we liked
them.

Our third visit to the United States was at the
time of the Civil War, and we could hardly
believe that it was the same country. Instead
of Pat and Hans being in disfavour with the
Sovereign People, they were on the very best of
terms. It was no longer, " D—n the Irish!
D—n the Dutch !" but " Welcome, my hearties !
The more there are of you the better. This is a
free country, where all men are equal, all eligible
for Government employ, all friends and brothers,
all save and except those never to be sufficiently
anathematized Southerners, out of whom it shall
be our united task to knock eleven bells." Food
for powder being wanted, the imported article
was in great demand. The next thing to strike
us was the increased number of our fellow
countrymen. On our former visits there were
apparently few English in the country ; no Irish,
or none, at least, who owned allegiance to Queen
Victoria. Now their name was legion ; and to

see the patriotic manner in which they kept
rushing to the British Consulates to declare
their nationality was very gratifying to one's
vanity as a liege man and true. Verily it is
only in the hour of peril that one can recognise
one's friends—more especially in the United
States. But it was not the aliens alone who
were patriotic. Every man, whether home-raised
or imported, was bursting with patriotism. The
free and enlightened citizen who did not feel
equal to the hardships of a campaign (the number
of weaklings was startling), and who had money,
purchased a substitute. No weakly soldier should
Uncle Sam have under his glorious star-spangled
banner, but the very best and stoutest men that
money could procure. What is money when the
very existence of one's country is at stake? They
were patriotic on principle. The remaining
portion of the population—the alien and non-
combatant—were patriotic, because it was their
interest to be so. They were, of course, at liberty
to have Southern proclivities if they pleased—
was it not a free country? But they didn't please,
and they showed their wisdom. " If you are not
the strongest, be the friend of the strongest," was
their motto; and so they hung out their bunting,
and shouted, " The Union, one and indivisible,"
until they were hoarse. What with principle on the

one hand and interest on the other, the country was having a " high old time" of it just then.

On our third visit to the United States we learnt that the Republican maxim, " The right of all governments is derived from the consent of the governed," applies only to such governments as are unable *vi et armis* to enforce their behests. That in model democracies as in effete autocracies, " Right is ever the might of the strongest." That in a free country a man can think as he likes, say what he likes, live how he likes, only so long as he thinks, and speaks, and lives according to the sovereign will and pleasure of that particular party which chances to be, for the time, in a political majority ; and lastly, that peculation, intimidation, and corruption are not incompatible with pure republicanism.

Our last visit to the United States was paid three years since. It is no longer of the past, but of the present we are writing.

Great is the progress that the country has made since the termination of the Civil War. When we call to mind the United States of eighteen years ago we can only rub our eyes and cry, *"Prodigious!"* New York has not been distanced in the race—she is more the " Empire City" than ever. She has enlarged her borders, built her palaces, made her parks. The city can no longer

be described as " built on the south end of
Manhattan Island, at the junction of the Hudson
and the East River," for New York is the Island
of Manhattan, the Island of Manhattan is New
York. What was Up-town in 1854 is Down-
town in 1871. The Astor House hotel yields
the *pas* to the Fifth Avenue. The Battery, the
Bowling Green, Washington Square, the City
Hall Park, St. John's Park, Grammercy Park,
all hide their diminished heads ; there is but one
park now---the Central. Palatial hotels can be
counted by the dozen, white marble stores by
the score, brown stone mansions by the hundred.
Evidences of the city's wealth abound on every
side—millionaries are " thick as leaves in
Valombrosa." Fortunes are no longer amassed
by long years of toil and thrift and self-denial,
as in the humdrum days of Stephen Girard and
Jacob Astor ; they are made at a stroke. One big
government contract, one lucky speculation, one
desperate *coup*, one gigantic swindle, and the
trick is done—the insolvent of yesterday, becomes
the millionaire of to-day. Not only has New
York increased in size, population, wealth, but
in expensiveness. On our first visit we had no
reason to be dissatisfied with our weekly bills.
The tariff at the Astor House was, if we remember rightly, two dollars per diem, a reduc-

tion being made to boarders by the month.   At
the second-class hotels the charge was one dollar
fifty cents, and in private houses good board was
obtainable for from six to eight dollars a week.
For half a dollar one could dine very fairly.
Now the charge at the larger hotels is five, and
even six dollars per diem, and at the second-class
three dollars.   Decent board cannot be had under
fourteen dollars a week, nothing resembling a
dinner for less than a dollar.   There are only
two things which are really cheap, newspapers
and oysters, the latter at twenty-five cents the
plate, being very cheap—cheaper, and much more
digestible than are even the newspapers, at one
cent the copy.

Notwithstanding the dearness of everything,
there seems to be no lack of buyers.   Where
does the money come from?   By charging more
for his wares, the merchant can certainly balance
his ledger, but how do non-traders manage—
employés of every description, whose salaries are
only just sufficient to procure them the necessaries
of life?   It was only after much patient in-
vestigation that we became possessed of this
wonderful secret—a secret which is well known
to every American, let him deny it as he will.
To our inquiry—" How do you manage to spend
half-a-crown upon sixpence a day?" the whispered

answer was—" Well ! we knock down some"—
in plain English peculate. Peculation is the
order of the day in the United States. The
chief encourager of peculation is no less a
personage than Uncle Sam himself, for by refusing to engage his servants for a longer term than
four years, he drives them into dishonest practices.
The employé who knows that he will be sent
about his business at the next general election,
is not likely to be a very faithful one. There
being no premium for honesty, he thinks he may
just as well be dishonest, and feather his nest
whilst he has the chance. The worst that can
befall him is to be dismissed before the expiration
of his term, and the plunder to be secured is
worth the risk. And so he knocks down whenever he has the chance, and millions of dollars
destined for Uncle Sam's strong-box, find their
way into the breeches' pockets of his subalterns.

The servants of the different public companies
follow suit. Railway and street-car conductors,
omnibus drivers, steamboat clerks—nearly every
man who is in such a position of trust that he
can peculate, does so.

"How do you manage it ?" we asked the ex-
conductor of a street railway-car. "Surely the
Company must be aware that they are being
robbed ?"

"Oh yes! No doubt of that."

" Well ?"

"They employ men to count how many passengers we carry each trip."

" And then ?"

" We spot the spotters, and make it all square with them." So that in America, to "set a thief to catch a thief" is a losing game.

In private concerns, where the master's eye is everywhere, " knocking down" may not be quite so easy a matter ; but on a smaller scale it can, we are informed, be generally managed by any man who is "smart;" and the American tradesman who can say truthfully that he is never robbed of a cent, has every reason to consider himself a remarkably wide-awake individual. We know not whether American business men add a certain percentage for black-mail to their tare and tret accounts, but we imagine they must do so in order to balance their ledgers. And that reminds us of a couple of stories, which will give the reader a better idea of how the oracle is worked across the water than would a folio of facts and figures. The stories may not be new, but they are to the point.

At a meeting of a certain railway board one of the directors moved for the summary dismissal of one of the conductors on the line, on the ground that he was robbing the Company.

Entering the service of the Company without a
" red cent" wherewith to bless himself, he had,
in little over a year, managed to purchase a
house, a 2-40 nag, a gold chronometer and
" fixings," a diamond ring and pin, and other
costly articles too numerous to mention. His
salary being only sixty dollars a month, it was
morally impossible that he could have saved sufficient in the time to pay for the horse, let alone
the other items. Where did the money come
from, if not out of the coffers of the Company?
He moved that the man be dismissed.

Upon this up rose another director to show
cause why the motion should be negatived. He
did not for one moment deny that the man was
a thief, but what would the Company gain by
dismissing him? It would be only changing
one thief for another thief, for they were all
thieves; and better a known evil than an
unknown ill. Besides, the conductor in question
had already made his pile. He had house, horse,
watch, ring, pin—was completely set up in fact;
if a reasonable man, he ought to be contented.
A new hand, on the contrary, would *have all
these things to buy;* and he therefore moved
that the man be retained, and retained he was
accordingly.

The other story is told of a man who purchased the good-will of a bar in one of the leading thoroughfares. On entering into possession he engaged at high wages a barkeeper renowned in the trade as a concocter of seductive drinks—cobblers, juleps, and such like, dear to the American palate. At first everything went along swimmingly—the bar was always full, the barkeeper's hands were never idle. A most invaluable servant was he, for " eye-openers," " gum-ticklers," and " corpse-revivers;" there wasn't his ditto in New York. Everything went along swimmingly, until it came to taking stock, when it was found that the balance was on the wrong side of the ledger; and so considerable was the deficit that nothing remained but to sell the business and compound with the creditors. The business was purchased by the accomplished barkeeper, who, out of pure compassion, consented to engage his late master as assistant. In less than a twelvemonth the new proprietor was, in his turn, insolvent; and on the business being offered for sale, it was repurchased by its former owner. Once again the accomplished barkeeper begged to be engaged, but a deaf ear was turned to his petition. " Guess, friend, we're about square," was the response. " I've learnt how eye-openers and gum-ticklers are concocted, and mean for the future to keep bar myself."

We often wonder whether those of our fellow-countrymen who are always panegyrizing American institutions, and disparaging those of their native land, have any idea of what it is they are speaking—whether they are ignorant or perverse, or both. How Americans must laugh in their sleeve to hear that Transatlantic morality has been made the subject of encomium at this or that meeting in the Old Country, and that they themselves have been held up by sedate members of the British Parliament as models for the rising generation! We can imagine the astonishment of Fifth Avenue on reading the following high-falutin sentence put into the mouth of the late Emperor of the French by a Yankee interviewer —"In your country the people submit to the law; and public sentiment, based upon general intelligence and morality, dictates and controls society." In your country the people submit to the law! It is for this reason, we presume, that men go armed as if they were in an enemy's country; that the troops have to be called out for the protection of inoffensive citizens; that the law of Judge Lynch so often supersedes the law of the land; that notorious malefectors walk

about the city in broad daylight; and that when
a murderer or desperado is brought to trial the
chances are that he escapes, because it would be
as much as the witnesses' lives are worth to give
evidence against him. " Public sentiment, based
upon general intelligence and morality, directs
and controls society," sounds very well; but will
any American dare to assert that the statement
is borne out by facts?

The United States is a great country—a very
great country—of that there can be no doubt;
and were it merely a question of natural advantages and disadvantages, Canada and Australia
might almost be passed over; for there would be
only one land for the emigrant—whether gentle
or simple—the land of the Stars and Stripes; for
her natural advantages are unequalled — her
resources immense. But other matters besides
the natural resources of a country have to enter
into the calculations of the gentleman emigrant.
He must consider the people with whom he will
be brought into contact, the reception that he will
be likely to meet with, the form of government
under which he will have henceforth to live, and
many other questions of equal importance; and it
is when these little items are thrown into the scale
that the United States is found wanting. For
the poor labouring man of industrious habits the

United States is second to no country on the face
of the globe, and, with certain provisos, for the
shrewd business man of moderate capital likewise ;
but in the existing state of things the gentleman
emigrant, and more especially the married gentleman emigrant, will, we are assured, feel far more
at home in Canada than in any of the Northern,
Eastern, or Western States. Our reasons for
thinking so will appear as we proceed.

Of all the strange sensations in this sensational
world, perhaps the very strangest is that which
a man experiences upon finding himself regarded
as a foreigner in a land where his own mother
tongue is spoken. There is as yet but one country
where the Englishman can feel the sensation,
and that country is the United States. To the
Canadian, the Australian, the New Zealander,
John Bull is a fellow-countryman ; to the American he is a foreigner. It is as an alien, not as
a citizen, that the emigrant to the United States
will enter upon his labours, and if he be a wise
emigrant, he will, until such time as he shall
have received his naturalization papers, comport
himself with the humility befitting an outside
barbarian. That he will be naturalized, and at
the very earliest date allowable, we assume, as a
matter of course, for we presume him to be a
reasonable barbarian, which he would not be were

he to endeavour to combine English ideas with American usages. Whatever secret yearnings he may have for the Old Country, he will avowedly be an ardent admirer of American institutions—tall of talk when the greatness of Yankeedom is in question, brimful of pity for the played out aristocracies of the Old World. Instead of his motto being that of the *New York Albion*—" *Cœlum, non animum, mutant, qui trans mare currunt*," it will be " *Ubi bene, ibi Patria*." Although in his address to the farmers and planters of the United States the author of the " American Farm Book" speaks of agriculture as the " most healthful, the most useful, the most *noble* employment of man, husbandry is not so regarded by the majority of Americans." The author being an American, and therefore " smart," had no occasion to be told that the surest way to make his book appreciated was by putting his readers on the very best of terms with themselves from first go-off, and this he cleverly effected by styling farming the *most noble* employment of man. Had he been writing on the mineral resources of the country, instead of on the agricultural, he would no doubt have declared " ile-striking" to be the noblest of man's missions. Did he not do so it would evince a great want of tact, for if " soft words butter no

parsnips," neither do they "break any bones."
It is better to soft sawder than to abuse. But
because a man writes buncombe, that is no reason
why sensible men should believe it; and if the
reader thinks that Americans endorse Mr. Allen's
dictum, he is very much mistaken. Instead of
farming being a favourite occupation, it is one of
the very last to which the smart, well-educated
American will turn his hand. He is ready to
peddle books or Yankee notions, to "run" a
meeting-house, or a whisky-mill, to stump ora-
torize, or teach school—do anything and everything which demands energy and intelligence.
But turn farmer—not if he knows it. Digging
and delving and lackeying is the particular province of the benighted Irish and Germans—trade
and mechanics that of free-born Americans. That
there are hundreds of thousands of pure-blooded
Americans who live by farming is undeniable;
but they farm because they are not sharp enough
to trade, and the very instant they are in a position
to employ labour, they commit the heavier work
of the farm into the hands of Hans or Mickey.
They will run the threshing-machine and drive
the haymaker or reaper, but when it comes to
hoeing and digging, they knock off. Americans,
and American politicians on the canvass more
especially, are very fond of talking about the

dignity of labour. But there is labour and labour, and farm and household labour do not come within the meaning of the text. To the American there is nothing undignified in peddling clothes'-pegs, or in "drumming" for some Yankee Doctor Dulcamara; but there is in domestic service and in the heavier labours of the farm. Like the English barber, he likewise has his line of demarcation, and he draws it at lackeying and earth-grubbing. The natural consequence is that whilst the country is overrun with mechanics, clerks, and pedlars, it is almost impossible to get an intelligent "help." It is the same with the women. They have a strong antipathy to going out to service, and sooner than degrade themselves by performing housework, they will ruin their health over a sewing-machine, subsist on a crust, and live in a garret.

The reason why farming as a calling ranks below shopkeeping, "drumming," and peddling, is easily explained. It is not a very money-making business, that is not for America, where the cry is "Make money, make money, make money, honestly if you can; but make money at all hazards." To make a fortune out of the land requires time—more time than the majority of Americans are inclined to give in this high-pressure age. They prefer the chance of becoming a millionaire by trade or speculation to the certainty of a competency out of the land. Some men there are who derive large incomes from their grapes, their peaches, or their asparagus; but they can hardly be called farmers, still less the planters of the Southern States, who raise cotton, tobacco, rice, and sugar. When we speak of farming, we mean ordinary farming, the growth of roots, hay, and cereals, and the feeding and fattening of cattle. In the United States, are no gentlemen farmers. A few wealthy men have model farms *à la* Mechi, but they farm more for amusement than for profit, and are perfectly satisfied if they can clear expenses, which many of them do not. But enough of the farmers' social status in the United States. The immigrant must take things as he finds them, and if the agriculturist plays second fiddle to the trader, second fiddle he must be content to play. We cannot alter the law of precedence to suit the reader, but we can assist him in the choice of a location—point out to him the advantages and disadvantages of each State or territory, circumscribe the area of his researches. We have before us a map of the United States. Let us commence by making a sort of running commentary on each State in succession.

Beginning with the New England States,

there is—Maine, trading and lumbering; New Hampshire, manufacturing and sterile; Vermont, more adapted for grazing than farming; Connecticut, trading, manufacturing, and farming; Massachusetts, ditto; Rhode Island, ditto. Except in the Connecticut valley, and a few other favoured spots, these States offer few attractions to the farmer. The land is none of the best, and will only yield good crops under first-rate management.

Next in succession comes New York, the State of States, attractive alike to the merchant, the speculator, the farmer, and the man of leisure. New York is the first city—the real capital of the Republic, the centre of all business operations, the head-quarters of pleasure and fashion. For banking transactions she is the American Frankfort; for shipping, her Liverpool; for gaiety and amusement, her Paris. She is the Empire City, and in comparison with her Boston, Philadelphia, Baltimore, New Orleans, St. Louis, Cincinnati and Chicago are mere provincial towns. In New York State there is sufficient water-power to turn all the mills in Christendom; as a cute Yankee once remarked, "Where will you find such another water privilege as Niagara?" The finest wheat in the world is grown in the valley of the Genesee. There are no better dairy farms than those of Orange and Dutchess counties ; the hay crop of Western New York is double that of the Southern States. As a residence for the man of independent means she is unsurpassed. In no other State can so many desirable locations be found— Long Island, the banks of the Hudson, and East River; the valley of the Mohawk, Saratoga, Newport, Niagara, Lake George, Lake Champlain, and that splendid tract of country lying between Syracuse and Rochester.

After New York comes Pennsylvania, another fine agricultural State, and settled by an orderly, hard-working race who, although mostly German by descent, have no aversion to foreigners, unless it be to the Irish. Not only is it a fertile, but an exceedingly picturesque State, and there are few more lovely valleys than those of the Susquehanna, Cumberland, Wyoming, and Kittatinny.

New Jersey and Delaware do not rank as first-class agricultural States. Their soil is light and sandy, and more adapted for fruit and vegetables than for hay and cereals. But many of the New Jersey market gardeners are wealthy men, whilst the Delaware peach-growers rank as planters, some of them netting twenty thousand dollars and upwards annually by the sale of their fruit alone.

Maryland is a fine little State, with a good climate and a good market—Baltimore—but for all that not to be compared to her elder sister Virginia. Of all the States in the Union, New York not excepted, Virginia is the one which would, we think, be most likely to suit the gentleman emigrant. Not only has she a fine climate, a fertile soil, good markets and numerous railways, rivers and navigable creeks; but what is perhaps of more importance to the gentleman emigrant than anything else, he would be certain of a cordial reception. His nationality, instead of being against him, would be decidedly in his favour. The F.F.V.s,* who boast their descent from cavalier and courtier, have always had English proclivities, and these proclivities have, since the war, developed into undisguised admiration. They think that they were badly treated by England, but they have forgiven her; and even if they have not, their hatred of the North is such that they have none left to bestow on her if they would. There would be no difficulty in finding a farm, for what with the war and the subsequent emancipation of the slaves, the planters are well nigh ruined, and there is hardly a man amongst them who is not desirous of selling a part of his estate.

* First Families of Virginia.

Further South than Virginia we need not go.
To the Carolinas, Georgia, Florida, Alabama,
Mississippi, Louisiana, Tennessee, and Arkansas
there is the insuperable objection that they con-
tain large free negro populations. We have been
in Hayti, and when we think what the Southern
States may one day become through negro as-
cendancy, we shudder. There is no shutting
our eyes to the fact that, whilst the negro's good
qualities are negative, his bad ones are positive.
He is not unintelligent, he is far from being ir-
religious, he is not incapable of affection; but he
is cruel, vindictive, sensual, obstinate, conceited,
and acts from impulse rather than from ratiocina-
tion. Should the coloured population ever get
the upper hand in any of the Southern States,
an event which is far from improbable, the
whites would have to leave. There would be no
living in the same house with them; for when
Massa Sambo becomes oberseer, we know how
he lays on the lash. If at this early stage of the
proceedings he gives himself airs, and endeavours
to lay down the law to the white folk, his late
masters, what will he do at a later? If he is in-
solent as a labourer, what will he be as a landed
proprietor? That a landed proprietor he will
one day become is pretty certain. When working on his own account, few men pile up the dol-

lars faster. For money-making he has a peculiar
aptitude. We do not suppose that he would
distinguish himself as a merchant or a stock-
broker, for he has not the necessary foresight ;
but as a small trader, as a huckster, publican, or
eating-house keeper, there are few to equal him.
Obtuse in some things, he is particularly wide awake
in others. No man knows better on which side his
bread is buttered. He is shrewd enough to
see that in the North it is not the farmer whose
work is the lightest, and whose profits are
the greatest, and he will therefore have
nothing whatever to do with the tillage of the
soil. He leaves that to "de poor Irish and
German trash, who knows no better." "Where
de work am light, and de prog am good, dat am
de place for Sambo." In the large hotels, where
his duties are confined to " doin' de honors ob de
dining-roob for de uppah ten ;" in the kitchen,
where there is a pleasant aroma of cooking,
and a fire at which he can warm his shins ; in the
bar, where he can concoct for himself iced
drinks in summer and spiced drinks in winter,
and, above all other places, in the barber's
saloon, where he can take the white man by the
nose and talk to him of "dis-yeah diborce case,
or dat-dah murdah"—Sambo is in his proper
sphere—in his Northern sphere. His sphere

down South is on a plantation, not as field hand, but as master. To own land, to become a planter, to be able in his turn to damn his niggers, and make them "hurry up," is the emancipated slave's ambition ; to attain that coveted position many negroes and mulattos are now working hard, and living frugally. Congenital laziness will prove too much for most of them, but some will undoubtedly succeed. They will become the owners of the land which once they tilled, and if any one desires to know what sort of a man is the negro planter, he has only to go to Hayti.

For our own part, sooner than live on terms of equality with such beings, we would sell our property for whatever it might fetch and clear out, and that is what we fear many white men will elect to do. Taking into consideration this probable exodus of the whites, it may be almost assumed that before the close of the century the blacks will far outnumber the whites in many of the more Southern States, and then—why, then Dixie will be neither more nor less than a second edition of Hayti. It was only a few days since that we were reading an account of a scene in a South Carolina Court House where the judge, the advocates, and the jury, all men of colour, were engaged in trying a white man for some petty misdemeanor. Had we been the culprit, we should have performed the "Happy Dispatch." We have no particular aversion to Sambo so long as he keeps his proper place; but to see him seated in judgment, that is coming it a little too strong.

The negro question has been shelved, not settled. It has already been the cause of one cruel war, it may cause another. There is no getting rid of it. Sambo is the stolen leg of mutton of which the purloiner cannot get rid— the hunchback who is always tumbling down the chimney. He cannot be hid away out of sight nor be passed off on pantaloon, nor can any one be coaxed to take charge of him. Whilst he was still a slave, he might possibly have been re-transported to his native Africa; but now that he is a free man it is out of the question. He can't be bribed to take his departure; he is perfectly contented with Dixie. He can't be prevented from increasing and multiplying and filling the land—is he not a man and a brother? He is the blackest cloud on the political horizon.

Returning northwards there is Ohio, a fine agricultural State, with good markets and ample rail and water communication. But with all its advantages, and they are many, Ohio is not the State we should be inclined to select as a residence. The climate of the northern portion of the State differs little from that of New York, and of the southern from that of Western Virginia, whilst in the vicinity of the rivers low fever is very prevalent. Land is almost as dear as in the neighbouring States of New York and Pennsylvania—much dearer than in Virginia—it is far from the sea board, and not sufficiently handy to New York, which is and must ever remain the Empire City. Lastly, we do not like the Buckeyes, as the inhabitants of the State are called, nearly as well as the New Yorkers, Pennsylvanians, and Virginians.

To Michigan there is the objection, that whilst the climate is just as severe as in Canada West, and the land neither better nor cheaper, the taxes are heavier and the luxuries of life much dearer than they are across the water. We cannot see the pull of settling in the dominions of Uncle Samuel when close at hand greater advantages are to be had, and at a cheaper rate, in the dominions of Queen Victoria. The same applies to Minnesota and the northern part of Indiana, Illinois, Iowa, and Wisconsin.

Little need be said of the Western States. The Free West is a sort of Irish-German reserve, where the emigrant's nationality would be decidedly against him, still more his social status.

He would be hated by his Irish neighbours, and not particularly loved by the German portion of the community. The English labouring man, if not received with any very great amount of cordiality, is at least tolerated by the Celtic population, for although a Saxon he has been to a great extent a fellow-sufferer. He, too, has had his being blighted by the "cold shade of the British aristocracy." But an English gentleman! Why, his presence would have the same effect upon them as has a red rag on a bull, and there would be a general shaking of heads and stamping of hoofs whenever he made his appearance. His features, his voice, his manner would remind them of my lord's agent of the inspector of police of the —— gauger, on the like of whom they had hoped never to set eyes again. The Germans, on the other hand, being unable to distinguish Celt from Saxon, would put him down as "von tam Irishmans," and when Hans prays to be delivered from the World, the Flesh, and the Devil, he adds, fervently, "*und die Irländer.*" The Irish would detest him because he was English, the Germans because he was Irish, and they would both hate him for being a gentleman born and bred.

But it is not for this reason alone that we counsel the gentleman emigrant to steer clear of the Western States. Rapid as has been the march of civilization, the country is, in most respects, still a long way behind the Northern, Eastern, and Middle States. Except in the longer-settled districts, and in the immediate vicinity of the different lines of railway, the roads are bad, and the towns and villages very " one-horse" places indeed. To look at the map one would certainly imagine that Iowa, Nebraska, Missouri, and all the Western States were thickly settled; so many are the roads, so numerous the cities, towns, and villages. But there are roads and roads, cities and cities, towns and towns; and when a high road is nothing more than a piece of corduroy laid across a swamp or a blazed line through a forest—when a saw-mill, black-smith's shop, store, church, school, and half a dozen frame houses are dubbed "city," and the respective shanties of Messrs. Byrne and Schmidt —Byrneville and Schmidtstown—it is astonish-ing how far a little civilization can be made to go —on the map. That all the luxuries of life are to be had in Chicago, and the other great Western cities, matters very little to the settler whose capital is limited to a few thousand pounds. So they are, and in a greater degree, in New York, Philadelphia, and Baltimore. But in one place, as in the other, they have to be paid for.

The only inducement to settle in the far west is
the comparative cheapness of land, and cheap
land is not to be had in the vicinity of these
great cities. The emigrant who wants cheap
land must go far a-field to look for it—miles
back from the older railways or on some new
line. The further it is from a railway, the
cheaper it will be; but so much heavier, likewise, will be the cost of sending produce to
market and of obtaining supplies. It is all very
well to be told that land in this or that township is selling for two dollars an acre. Unless
there is a market handy, it would be dear at a
gift. Cheap land, as we have already had occasion to remark, will be found, in nine cases out
of ten, a delusion and a snare. We mean that
the gentleman emigrant will so find it. To
Mickey, whose habitation in the Ould Counthry
was a mud cabin, and whose daily fare was
potatoes and buttermilk, and to Hans, reared on
sauerkraut and pumpernickel—the very fact of
owning land, and of having plenty to eat and
drink, is sufficient compensation for the loss of
home, friends, old habits, and associations. But
with the gentleman it is different. Never having
known the pangs of hunger, he does not fall into
ecstasies over his bread and butter, and the
eternal pork and beans of the West; nor does he

feel particularly proud of his frame cottage, with its half section of wilderness or prairie. It is not sufficient that he has a roof to cover him, and plenty to eat and drink. He yearns for companionship; for a more advanced state of civilization than he sees around him; for those thousand and one little *agrémcnts* of refined society which, costing nothing in the older States, are not to be procured in the newly settled districts of the West at any price.

That the West is the " poor man's paradise" we do not deny, but it is a paradise which has been very much over-rated. The Yankee speculator or agent for railway land grants, whilst expatiating on the immense superiority of prairie over all other descriptions of country, wisely ignores many serious drawbacks which the prairie farmer has to encounter. On the boundless plains of the Great West, the settler, we are told, has not to " battle with the forest" as in other less favoured districts—North, East, and South. The land lies ready prepared for the hand of the sower, and he has only to go in and win. " That's so," no doubt. But if he have no trees to cut down, neither has he any wherewith to build his shanty, nor yet for fencing or fuel. If clearing cost him nothing, or next to it, house-building does, as likewise his fencing and his

firing.   The prairie farmer has no clearing to do
worth mentioning; and so, as a natural consequence, there can be no spruce logs for a shanty,
nor any saw-mill where he can purchase timber
at ten dollars a thousand.   He can, of course,
live in a hovel, or burrow in the ground like a
prairie dog; but if he wants a decent house he
must get his building materials from the less
favoured districts lying to the northward or
eastward of his Canaan, or else arrange to have
his house sent to him all ready-made from
Chicago or other large town.   The last plan is
perhaps the best and the cheapest; but it is
expensive at the best.   In their charges for the
transport of produce and merchandize, the different railway companies do not err on the side
of moderation.   They sell the land on each side
the track at a comparatively low figure; but
when Mr. Settler is nicely settled, and wants to
send his produce to market, they lay it on.
They lay it on to such effect that, in many
places, it takes the value of two bushels of corn
to send the third to market; but then we are
told that the said corn makes excellent fuel—
"Six acres of it will keep a family in fuel the
entire winter."   Happy land, where corn is so
abundant that it takes the place of coal and cord-
wood !

And then the beauty of the prairies!—one immense verdant expanse undisfigured by tree or mountain—beautiful in the summer, when the fierce western sun is blazing over head, thrice beautiful in the winter, when the wind, unchecked by forest or mountain, comes sweeping along with such fury that the settler's frame house shakes and quivers like a vessel in an Atlantic gale. But it is a fine country for the poor man. Has he not plenty to eat and drink, and corn in abundance for his beasts, and his stove? What more can he desire?

Before the gentleman emigrant takes up prairie land, let him pass a winter at some settler's house in the vicinity of the lot he intends to purchase. The prairie in summer is one thing, the prairie in winter another.

The West may be the poor man's paradise, but for the gentleman emigrant there are many more desirable locations. Even supposing that he should decide upon settling in one of the Western States, he ought never to invest his entire capital in an improved farm. It is not by farming that a man may hope to become a millionaire, but by speculating. He should watch his opportunity, and the instant a new line of railway is projected, and the track marked out, buy up land along it. The promoters would of

course appropriate the best lots, but by a
little judicious palm-greasing he will have no
difficulty in securing a fair share of the plunder.
With ordinary caution and judgment he will
run little risk. He will only have to wait two—
three—five years, according to the influx of
population, to sell out at a considerable profit.
There will be no necessity to cut down a single
tree, nor to put up a rod of fencing. The lots
once inspected, he may leave them until the time
comes for selling. The land cannot fly away;
there will be no fear of Nature stopping payment.
In a word, judicious land speculation is much
more profitable than any farming.

If the Western States are not suited to the
gentleman emigrant, neither are the territories,
for as Iowa, Nebraska, Minnesota, and Wisconsin
are the head-quarters of Irish and German immigrants, so are Colorado, Dakotah, Nevada,
Montana, and Idaho those of adventurous spirits
and desperadoes. If it be his desire to turn
gambusino, or to invest his capital in mining
operations, then undoubtedly the territories are
his best head-quarters; but if to farm be his
intention, they may be passed over as ineligible.

On the Pacific slope there is California, a great
agricultural State, for a nugget with pick and
shovel saltier is no longer her escutcheon, but a

cornucopia. As a wheat-producing State, she ranks, we believe, fourth; as a fruit-producing, first. In the valleys of Lower California, the vine, the orange, the lime, the lemon, the fig, and the olive grow luxuriantly, and when properly cultivated yield an abundant harvest, whilst her wheat crop, both for quality and quantity, is unsurpassed. In years gone by, the Californian fruit grower had some difficulty in disposing of his produce, but since the opening of the Pacific railway, that bar to his success has been to a great extent removed. In less than a week his crop is whisked by the iron horse from Pacific to Atlantic, and Californian grapes and figs and oranges may now be seen in every fruiterer's window. Day by day the demand for Californian fruit is increasing, and it does not require a vast amount of inspiration to predict that the Golden State is destined to become, at no distant date, the forcing house, if not the vineyard of Uncle Samuel. But apart from fruit growing and viniculture, California would not seem to offer a single advantage which cannot likewise be found in several of the more accessible States, whilst she has some disadvantages which are peculiarly her own.

We say that she does not *seem* to possess, for never having crossed the Rocky Mountains we are not in a position to speak authoritatively. We have no wish to pretend to more knowledge of our subject than we really possess, nor that this, our treatise on emigration, should be a salmagundi concocted from the experiences and writings of others. They only are omniscient, they only can write ex cathedrâ whose travels are confined to the shelves of Mudie's library, or who can only just spare the time for a two months' scamper across a continent.

If California have a fine climate, so has Virginia; if she be a great wheat-producing State, so is New York; if her winters are milder and her springs earlier than are those of the Northern and Eastern States, so likewise are the springs and winters of every State lying south of the Potomac. On the other hand, labour is scarce and dear in California; the country is inundated with Celestials, who, if good servants, are the least desirable of emigrants, whilst all the Pacific railways that can be constructed will not bring San Francisco one yard nearer to New York, nor shorten the distance to market. The Californian market-gardener can never compete successfully with the Virginian and the Floridan, for though it may pay to send choice fruits 3500 miles to market, it would hardly answer to send peas and tomatoes.

Oregon being still a young, sparsely settled State, offering few advantages to the emigrant, and Alaska, Uncle Sam's latest acquisition, still fewer, we can leave the Pacific slope and fold up our map, for having passed all the States in review; we can now proceed to the task of selection.

Rejecting the North-Eastern States on account of the poverty of the soil and the severity of the climate, the North-Western because they have nothing to offer which Canada cannot offer likewise, the Southern (Maryland and Virginia accepted) because of their negro population, and the Western as being neither more nor less than a great Irish-German reserve, we find that we have but six States remaining — New York, Ohio, Pennsylvania, New Jersey, Maryland, and Virginia.

Let us preface our remarks on New York by observing that it is not a good State for the needy man. It is only to the monied emigrant that New York offers any special attraction or advantage. The man whose capital is limited to a few thousand pounds, who is not in a measure independent of his farm, would do well to choose a less pretentious State. Of what advantage are large cities, gay watering-places, fashionable society, if poverty compel one to stay at home?

Living is expensive in New York State, and land commands a high price, that is, land in favourite localities, for we do not suppose that the gentleman who selected the Empire State as a residence would care to bury himself in the wilderness— for a wilderness there is, and an extensive one. He would require a farm in a picked spot—on the banks of the Hudson, in Orange, Dutchess, or West Chester counties, in the Valley of the Genesee, on one of the northern lakes—Skancatless, Owasco, Cayuga, or Seneca. Were money no object, and we desirous of settling in the State of New York, we should certainly select one of the three counties we have mentioned—Orange, Dutchess, or West Chester. All three are within easy reach of the City; they are splendid grazing counties, and if dairy farming can be made to pay anywhere in the State, it should pay there —Orange, Dutchess, and West Chester butter, and all dairy produce, fetching the top price in the market. The country is most picturesque, and in the highest state of cultivation; the roads are excellent; and lastly, there is better society, and more of it than in any other section of the State. Nothing can, to our mind, be more perfectly lovely than the banks of the Hudson. No spot on Rhine or Danube surpasses in beauty the bend of the river at West Point, more especially in the fall of the year, when the mountain side is one mass of brilliant colouring. But one thing is wanting—the mellowing impress of the past.

The annals of West Point date from yesterday. Never did steel-clad knight sally from its fortress, nor had freebooter ever his stronghold on the opposite hill. Neither is "Anthony's Nose" associated with a hermit, nor the "Crow's Nest" with a brigand, nor the "Highlands" with the exploits of an American Rob Roy. In West Point annals figure but two historic names —Washington and Kosciusko. There are those who affect to despise ruins, and who turn into ridicule every story that is not founded on fact. But we are not of them; and the absence of mouldering abbey and ruined castle, of all legends, traditions, and fairy tales, is to us the greatest drawback to the enjoyment of American scenery.

The great bar to settling in what may be called the Home Counties, is the exorbitant price demanded for first-class farms. Land is just as dear as in Kent or Surrey—in some picked spots dearer. From inquiries we made in the neighbourhood of Goshen, in Orange County, and of Poughkeepsie, in Dutchess County, we are convinced that to commence farming in those localites, as much capital would be required as at home, whilst the profit to be derived therefrom would be little, if anything, in excess of that made by the English farmer. Such being the case, in what respect, the reader will naturally inquire, would a man be the gainer by emigrating? If land be as dear as in England, and the profits to be derived from farming no greater, why not stay at home?

At first glance the gain is not very apparent, we admit; but a gain there is for all that. In the first place, notwithstanding the severity of the winter, the climate is better than in England. Secondly, the man who has his wits about him can obtain a much higher rate of interest for his money than he can at home. Thirdly, he is no longer a slave to appearances. He can live as he "durned pleases," and, the cod-fish aristocracy excepted, no one will think the better or the worse of him, whether he entertain like a prince or vegetate like an anchorite. It is only when a man runs for office or takes a prominent part in politics, that his private affairs become public property. Fourthly, to enjoy a little shooting or fishing, it is not necessary to hire a moor or a salmon river. It costs no more to go from New York to Maine, New Bruswick, Nova Scotia, the Adirondacks, or the Thousand Islands, than it does from London to Aberdeen, and when one gets there, two or three dollars a day for guide and boat is all that shooting and fishing need cost one. Even buffalo hunting and prairie chicken shooting can be had at a trifling outlay. Iowa and Kansas are distant States; but the fare there and back would not amount to a tenth part of the sum paid for a third-class moor in Scotland. In order to have sport, it is not necessary that one live in the wilderness. *The Cedars*, the residence of the late H. W. Herbert (Frank Forrester) was in the neighbourhood of Newark, New Jersey. We should pitch our wigwam on Long Island sound or on the banks of the Hudson. Many happy hunting grounds would be within a day's journey, and we should have yachting and fishing on the spot. Yachting is now an American "institution," and during the summer months the bay and the sound are alive with white-winged craft of all rigs and sizes. And right sociable fellows are the yachtsmen. Let the Britisher only shake off his insular prejudices and endeavour to make himself agreeable, and he will have no lack of invitations to take a cruise. And it is not the yachtsmen alone who are sociable. Grateful for many a kindness received at their hands, we can say, conscientiously, that no people are, when at home, more sociable, more hospitable, or warmer-hearted than the Americans. Whatever may be

Jonathan's failings, no one can accuse him of stinginess. As a trader, he is close; as a man, he is open-handed; and the same Yankee who would be miserable were you to get the better of him to the amount of one dollar, will think nothing of giving you a dinner that costs him twenty. The English traveller, whose experiences of the American people have been picked up in hotels, steamers, and railway cars, is apt to form a very erroneous opinion of the national character, for the American's worst qualities are on the surface, his best lie hidden beneath. We speak of the well-educated, pure-blooded American, not of the upstart and half-bred.

Whilst out on his travels he is the irrepressible American pilgrim whom we all know so well—loud-spoken, self-sufficient, dictatorial, contradictory, feverishly impatient to impress every one with a due sense of his wealth and importance, whilst in his public capacity of city councilman or alderman, or what not, he is irritable, quarrelsome, and, perhaps, a little vindictive. His journeyings over, his toga laid aside, and once again beneath his own roof-tree, Jonathan is another man. He is no longer the bragging, dictatorial American pilgrim, the irascible, blustering demagogue, but the unassuming, affable gentleman—a devoted husband, an indulgent father, a kind and considerate friend, and a worthy good fellow in every respect. Before the public he is acting a part; it is only when at home that he is natural. And whilst we are still in New York, the head-quarters of shoddy, a few words on the "cod-fish" aristocracy of the Empire City.

Great wealth being incompatible with republican simplicity, that attempts at aristocratic exclusiveness should have been made by some *nouveaux riches* is not surprising. What is the good of having money if it does not place one on a better social footing than one's poorer neighbours? And so there arises an "Upper-tendom" —a monied aristocracy like that which one sees to-day in New York. On our first visit to Gotham, the nearest approach to a livery was a black velvet band round Sambo's hat and plain silver buttons on his overcoat. Now livery is an American institution and armorial bearings are beginning to make their appearance on the panels of the "bong-tong barouches" of the fashionables. Nay, if we are not greatly mistaken, there is a self-dubbed herald in Broadway who emblazons arms and traces pedigrees *secundum artem*, or according to Cocker. It is surprising how he survives it, for in the exercise of his calling he has to clear generations-centuries at a bound, and there is a limit to even a herald's elasticity. It is impossible to ignore the existence of Mr. Shoddy, for he takes care that his comings and goings, his wealth and his splendour, shall be constantly before the public. He pays newspaper reporters to write flaming descriptions of his "palatial" abode — all New York — all America must know the treasures that his mansion contains, and what he gave for everything. The furniture imported from Paris direct, the wines from the banks of Rhone and Garonne, the pictures—Raphaels, Titians, Correggios (our friend is a connoisseur)—from Rome and Florence—everything of the very best and *of the very dearest.* Nothing is omitted from the priced catalogue. His trotting horses so much; his wife's diamonds, purchased from Tiffany, so much; his daughters' wardrobes so much—all are made the subject of special laudation; and in the event of one of the girls being married, the trousseau will be minutely described, from the young lady's bridal veil to her garters. Those who remember the "Diamond" and other celebrated New York weddings, will know if we state the truth. But the task of the American newspaper reporter does not end here. Not only is he an appraiser, but a pen-and-ink portrait painter into the bargain. He seizes upon such occasions as Mrs. De Morphie's *déjeûner*, or Mrs. Petrolia's ball, to trot out the families of his clients, and portrays Miss Theodosia's languishing eyes and snowy bosom, and Miss Evelina's golden locks and swan-like neck, with a freedom of touch worthy of a Titian or a Rubens.

But unless the emigrant have more money than most emigrants are blessed with, it is not probable that he will receive much attention from these republican aristocrats—money or a handle to his name. Rank has now a value in the Gotham matrimonial market—a prince so many thousand dollars, a count so many, a baron so many, and, be it remarked, *en passant*, that the foreign nobility take care that it shall be *cash down*. No need for the titled *émigré* to turn farmer—ignorant or talented, ugly or handsome, profligate or virtuous, matters not a straw—he will experience no difficulty in finding a wife and a fortune.

If we had not the money to purchase a farm in the district we have named, and a surplus sufficient to enable us to live independently of the profits to be derived from farming, we should, presuming that it was New York State or nothing, select the country lying between Syracuse and Canandaigua—most probably on one of those five lakes before mentioned—Skancatless, Owasco,

Cayuga, Seneca, or Canandaigua. Were we free to settle where we pleased, we should not think of looking for a "location" between Poughkeepsie and Niagara, but cross over into Canada; for although northern New York is a splendid farming country, picturesque, thickly settled, with good roads, and markets innumerable, it has little to offer to the emigrant which Canada cannot offer likewise, and when the advantages are equal, or nearly so, we prefer the Union Jack to the Yankee Gridiron. But tastes differ, and for those who prefer American institutions to British—who like Jonathan better than Jean François—there are, we admit, few more desirable districts, whether in the Empire or any other State, than that lying along the New York Central Railway. The great objection to settling in this and in every picked spot is, as we have already said, the excessive dearness of land. What with the present high rate of wages, the comparatively low prices now ruling for all descriptions of farm produce, and the taxes which the Government is obliged to levy in order to pay the interest of the national debt, the eastern farmer finds it no easy matter to make a living. There may be many farmers in New York and the neighbouring States whose lands have proved a mine of wealth, but we have not had the

pleasure of meeting any of them on our travels.
If they were making rapid fortunes, if they had
more money than they knew what to do with,
if their incomings exceeded their outgoings in any
marked degree, they "played possum" when
under our cross-examination. One and all had
the same story to tell. They made a fair living,
managed to lay by sufficient to start the boys in
some trade or business and portion off the girls;
but real rich they "rayther guessed they warnt."
And it must be borne in mind that the American
farmer is much more frugal than his English
brother. What he calls living the British
yeoman would call starving. On his board are
seen no big joints and unlimited home-brewed.
Ordinaries—such as those to which the English
farmer sits down every market-day—would seem
Epicurean feasts in his eyes. Except on high-
days and holidays—at Christmas, at "Thanks-
giving," or on a birthday, fresh meat is seldom
seen on his table. It is only in the vivid imagination of the "Emigrant Guide Book" compiler
that the table of the American farmer groans
beneath the weight of juicy sirloins, fat haunches,
and plump turkeys and capons. Year in, year
out—at breakfast, dinner, and supper—salt pork is
the standing dish—salt pork with variations. Salt
pork fried with potatoes—salt pork baked with

beans—salt pork boiled with cabbage—and pies and cakes of different degrees of indigestibility, the whole washed down with tea or iced water. The American farmer's market dinner costs him a quarter—one shilling. He would as soon think of ordering dissolved pearls as port or sherry—a bottle of spruce beer or a whisky "straight" is enough for him. If he is ever guilty of extravagance it is in the purchase of horse-flesh. He likes to have a pair of fast-trotting horses in his waggon, and would no more consent to drive the stamp of animal which drags Farmer Turmit's gig to market than he would consent to sit hour after hour with that worthy guzzling brandy-and-water in the bar-parlour of the Wheatsheaf or Red Lion.

A very homely humdrum life is that led by the American farmer. Amusement he has absolutely none. He is rarely a sportsman; he never plays cricket or foot-ball or bowls—even the national game of base-ball is at a discount in the country. As for dancing, he leaves that kind of capering to them silly foreigners who knows no better. When not at home, at meeting or at market, he is pretty certain to be found at the village store discussing the affairs of his neighbours and of the nation generally.

Jonathan junior takes after his sire. He

don't care much for gunning, or fishing, or riding, and guesses base-ball is sorter like hard work, of which he has more nor enough tew home. His off time is passed in acting as charioteer to his sisters on their shopping or visiting rounds, and in sheepishly "sparking" the girls at "bees" or singing skule; or, when not so employed, he will in all probability be found seated on a rail whittling, and recounting to some brother yokel the adventures which befell him when down to New York or Bosting. A great raw-boned, hard-fisted, good-natured youth is he, with as much grace about him as a snapping turtle.

The wives and daughters of American farmers bear about as much resemblance to English women of the same class as does a medlar to a pippin. The work which would seem mere child's play to the English farm wife would kill them outright. Their labours are of the lightest kind, and they take little or no exercise. They can neither fetch an armful of wood from the outhouse, nor draw a pail of water, nor milk the cows, nor churn the butter, nor do any work where physical strength is required. When wood or water is wanted, the chore boy has to fetch it. When they desire to attend singing school or meeting, the horses must be put into

the sleigh or waggon, to convey them the short
distance between their house and the village.
Their throne is a rocking-chair, and rocking
themselves the ostensible aim and end of their
existence. What with their rocking-chairs, hot
stoves, and hot drinks in winter, and their rocking-chairs, fans, and iced drinks in summer, the
lollipops and gum which they chew at all seasons,
and their hatred of outdoor exercise, they are, as
may be imagined, as weedy a lot as one would
desire to see. Always ailing, and dosing, and
pilling, the wonder is how they manage to pull
through at all.

But because the majority of American farmers
live in this stupid way, that is no reason why
sensible men should follow their example.
America is not Europe, neither is northern New
York the county of Kent; but for all that life
in the longer settled States is endurable—very
endurable indeed. Men there are, of course—
Anglo-Saxons and their descendants more especially—who, like certain ships, have a happy
knack of always making bad weather of it. As
in the one case the breeze is too light or too stiff
—the seas are too long or too short—so in the
other it is the climate that is bad, the land
which is poor, the people who are detestable.

To decide whether there be any reasonable

ground for such charges, one must know the antecedents of the complainant. Everything goes by comparison. If the plaintiff hail from a land where the "flowers ever blossom, the beams ever shine," and where one has only to "tickle the earth with a hoe to make it smile with a harvest," he is justified in saying that the climate of Canada and the Northern States is a severe one, and that nature is niggardly; and if he have been from infancy accustomed to the most refined and the most intellectual society, that the American people are, as a rule, somewhat rough and uncultivated. But of the great army of growlers, how many are there who can urge this plea in justification? So far as our experience goes, the number is exceedingly limited. It is not the best bred that are the most discontented, and, were inquiry to be made, it would be found that the growlers belong, not to the upper, but to the lower middle class, men whose experiences of the Sunny South have been picked up in the palm-house at Kew, and whose ideas of refined society are associated with the frequenters of the bar-parlour or commercial room of the principal inn in their native village.

That in the United States and the Canadas society is somewhat mixed, and that in most places it is far below the English average, we

have already admitted : it could not well be
otherwise.   But at its worst it is scarcely as
detestable as Canadian Owl and birds of his
feather would have us believe.   It must be
indeed a " remote township" where not a single
companionable being is to be found—not a man
who has received a liberal education.   In every
settlement worthy the name are pretty sure to
be found representatives of the three learned
professions.   A go-to-meeting race, Americans
must have their resident minister—a litigious
race, their lawyer—an ailing race, their doctor—
let the community be ever so small ; and if out
of the three the gentleman immigrant cannot
find one worthy of his friendship, he must be
either hard to please or have been exceedingly
unfortunate in his choice of a location.

To the University-educated Englishman the
erudition of these graduates in Transatlantic
Divinity, Law, and Medicine may seem small,
their manners uncouth, their knowledge of the
world exceedingly limited.   But then it is not
every man who is able to gauge his fellow-men
by English University standard, whose education and manners have received their finishing
touches on the banks of Cam or Isis ; and for
the vast majority of gentlemen immigrants the
society of American professional men is learned

and refined enough. They may not be able to
spout a Greek play, or to demonstrate algebraically
how many blue beans make five; but they can,
in plain English or in plain American, argue
eloquently and to the point, and prove that
two and three make five without the aid of
logarithms; whilst snugly stowed away, but
ready for use when wanted, they have generally
a fund of useful information such as few University-educated Englishmen possess. Different
countries different ways—different peoples different standards of excellence. Were all nations
to be measured by our British standard, there
would be but one perfect people on the face of
the earth—the English. We are not so English
as to be unable to find anything to like or admire
out of our own country; and to the many good
traits in the American character we can bear
testimony, and all the more cheerfully that we
have been rather too ready in pointing out the
bad ones.

Putting aside, then, all insular prejudice, and
viewing American professional men from a
cosmopolitan standpoint, we have no hesitation
in saying, that if inferior to their English *con-
frères* in science and culture, they are every whit
as companionable. The educated American is, as
a rule, an exceedingly companionable individual.

Once out of harness and on the " rampage," and whether the said rampage be in New York, or in the backwoods, or in the polar regions, he will be found " All thar', and no mistake." Exceptions there are, no doubt ; but, taking them one with another, better men for mess-mates we have never come across in our travels. Patient under privation, ready on an emergency, handy at all times—not eternally grumbling and growling like John Bull, nor uncertain of temper like Paddy, nor kicking his heels in the air *à la* Jean Crapaud—the American is a model *voyageur*. We use the French Canadian word, there being nothing synonymous in English. The Canadian voyageur is not a traveller in our English sense, but an explorer, a hunter, a trapper—a sojourner, not in hotels and caravansaries, but in shanties and wigwams—a man who can depend on his own rifle for subsistence, and eat his mocassins if that fail him—a man who can chop his own wood, build his own camp-fire, paddle his own canoe, and carry it—in a word, a thorough back-woodsman. With all due respect to the superior acquirements of Oxonians and Cantabs, we know whom we should select for our fellow-voyageur did our choice lie between one of their number and one of the many American professional men —lawyers and doctors with whom we have

camped out—not on the score of superior phy-
sique, but on that of superior sociability. We
warrant that, for every story the Englishman
had to tell, the Yankee would tell a score; for
every droll remark made by the one, a hundred
would be made by the other.

No need for the gentleman immigrant, who
purchases a farm in the vicinity of the New York
Central Railroad, to live like a recluse, or to
become a "watch-dog about his premises." If
he desire society, he can have it—not quite so
genteel perhaps as at home, but sufficiently good
for ordinary mortals. His life would not differ
much from that led by his brother immigrant
across the water in Canada. The climate being
very similar, busy and slack times would come
at the same seasons. Late spring, summer, and
early autumn would be his busy time—late
autumn and winter his slack. As to the profits
to be derived from farming in northern New
York, we can only repeat what we have said
respecting such profits in the Southern division
of the State. We have yet to find the man who
would own up to having made a fortune by the
tillage of the soil. They managed to make a
living, and were content—no, not exactly content—and they grumbled like farmers all the
world over. We would only remind the reader

once again that land, taxes, and labour are higher
—clothing and all the luxuries of life dearer—
than across the border; whilst the difference in
the value of farm produce seems hardly suffi -
cient to restore the balance. As regards the
remaining advantages and disadvantages of either
country, we may say that they are balanced, or
nearly so. The pleasures and tribulations of
Mr. Benedict, Ontario, and of Mr. Benedict,
New York State, would, if they were to compare
notes, be found surprisingly similar.

The ordinary country folk are as familiar and
as independent, the servants as bad and as
"sassy," in the one country as in the other,
whilst for amusements of every description there
is not a pin to choose between them. If Toronto
be further, New York and Boston are nearer,
whilst Niagara belongs to both. The better
classes in such towns as Auburn, Geneva, and
Canandaigua are just as well educated, and as
sociably inclined as they are in London, Wood-
stock, or Cornwallis, nor would the fact of the
new-comer being an Englishman lessen the
warmth of his reception. The sportsman will
find fin, fur, and feather within the precincts of
the State, and if he hanker after very big game
indeed, the happy hunting grounds, where roam
the bear, the bison, the moose, and the cariboo,

are as accessible to him as they are to the
Canadian. Presuming that he lived in the
vicinity of one of the towns we have named—
Auburn, Geneva, or Canandaigua—and three more
desirable residences it would be difficult to find;
he would have good fishing and fair duck shooting at his very door, and a run by rail of eighty
miles or so would bring him to the edge of the
great New York wilderness, where, notwithstanding the indiscriminate annual slaughter of
deer, in season and out of season, passable sport
is still to be found.

At the date of our first visit to the said wilderness, now some eighteen years ago, it was a
veritable huntsman's paradise. Easy of access,
and yet too far removed from the main lines of
travel, and too destitute of hotel accommodation,
to attract the feather-bed sportsmen of Boston
and New York—not overrun with game, but
with just sufficient to make the sport exciting—
with scenery charmingly diversified—hill, mountain, lake, and river—it was, black-flies and
mosquitoes excepted, all that the hunter's heart
could desire. Whether he struck into the woods
from North, South, East, or West—from
Chateauguay, Lake George, Port Kent, or
Martinsburg, he could depend upon having, not
only a " good," but a " high old" time. What

pleasant days we have passed in those woods!
How the old camping-grounds rise up before us
as we write! our shanty on upper Chateauguay,
on St. Regis, on Big Clear, on the Saranac, and
last, not least, on that nameless little pond
situated as nearly as possible in the heart of the
wilderness. Ah, that was a camp indeed! Not
as regards comfort, for the shanty had been
roughly put together, and was neither wind-
proof nor water-proof—not for the beauty of the
site, for there was nothing remarkable about it—
not for the sport we had there, for it was insig-
nificant—but for the jollity of our party. Our
three camp-mates—a doctor, a lawyer, and a
gentleman of the Fourth Estate—had come to the
woods with the express intention of having a
good time, and they had it. The "sound of
revelry by night" that for a month and more
issued from that shanty, must have driven every
right-minded owl, in our section of the wilderness,
raving mad. The soberest owl amongst them
could not have accused us of being dipsomaniacs,
for although a fair amount of liquor was con-
sumed, the pipe was more in requisition than the
glass—"Old Varginny" than "Bourbon." But
that our behaviour was scarcely in harmony with
the scene there is no denying. In the deep stillness of the woods a very little exertion of the

lungs suffices to awaken the echoes, and when the Doctor, who was a good performer on the cornet, favoured us with an *obbligato* accompaniment to some ringing chorus, it 'must doubtless have seemed to an outsider as if all the demons of the forest had broken loose.

On our first arrival, the Lawyer, who was elected by acclamation the captain of the party, or, in backwoods vernacular, " boss of the crowd,'' drew up, and affixed to the wall of the shanty the rules and regulations to be observed at the camp on Nameless Lake, which rules, notwithstanding an occasional growl on the part of the guides, were carried out to the letter. At daybreak each morning the guides turned out, and set about preparing breakfast. At sunrise a gruff summons from the cook roused the rest of the party. A wash, or header into the lake, according to our respective habits, and then breakfast. Breakfast over, a general distribution of forces according to the arrangements of the previous evening—some to fish, others to hunt, the cook alone remaining at the shanty.

Would that we could panegyrize the sportsmanlike qualities of our three friends in the same manner that we have praised their convivial. Alas! we cannot. Three greater pot-hunters could not have been found in the State of New

York. For the sake of game—game in its culinary sense—they would be guilty of any turpitude. Driving deer to water and night hunting was, in their eyes, perfectly legitimate sport—potting from a distance of fifteen paces some wretched ruffed grouse, perched on stump or branch, a feat of which to be proud. If poor "Frank Forrester" had been of the party, what a row there would have been in that shanty!

Pot-hunters though they were, they did not particularly distinguish themselves even in that capacity. One deer was murdered by them in an adjoining lake, and another they potted night hunting. At the deer, which the dogs drove to water, a dozen shots were fired before one took effect, and it was from the blow of an axe, and not from a bullet, that the poor brute finally received its death wound. We witnessed the entire performance from the shore, and kept thanking our stars the while that we were not of the party, for the bullets went ricocheting about in all directions, and the position of the hunters was, to say the least, "rayther permisc'ous." It was not the deer that was in the most danger, but the deer-slayers. In the night-hunting expeditions we took an active part, and if the deer had not ample notice of the approach of the boat, it was no fault of ours—our whispers could be heard half a mile off. The whole thing was as good as a play'.

We generally volunteered to paddle the Doctor, and when we fell in with deer, which was not always, the story of the night's work, as entered in our journal, would be something as follows :—

"Couple of hours before sundown start off with Doctor for —— Lake. Outlet of same, according to guides, 'first-rate' spot for night hunting. Find guide awaiting us with canoe. Arrived at outlet, run canoe ashore, and, whilst Doctor lights lamp, smoke pipe of reflection."

Very proud was the Doctor of that same lamp. Had the sport only been in proportion to the light it shed, not a deer would have been left alive in the wilderness. It had, if we remember rightly, six burners, whilst its plated reflector was as large and as bright as the shield of Achilles.

"Into canoe again, and down outlet—Doctor in bows, with neck craned forward and both ears cocked, peering into gloom, I paddling. No breeze stirring, not a sound to break stillness of night but rustle of lily-pads as canoe brushes past. Stop from time to time at signal from Doctor, who hears, or fancies that he hears, deer ahead. False alarms. Five minutes — ten minutes—fifteen minutes—two-thirds of the

distance covered—nothing. All at once frantic
motions from Doctor to stop. Back water
accordingly, and listen. Deer! and not far distant either. Doctor with hand on slide of lan-
tern, for showing light at once. Entreat him, in
stage whisper, to 'hold hard a minute,' and at
same time, in sending canoe ahead, make (acci-
dentally) slight noise with paddle. Doctor too
excited to hear it—deer do. A splashing of
water—a crashing of branches—— Off, by
thunder! Considerable swearing at one end of
the canoe—words of consolation and sympathy
from the other. Can't be helped. Nothing for
it but to return home. Better luck next time,"
&c. &c. &c.

Once, however, the Doctor proved too many
for us. He pulled down the slide at the right
moment, and knocked over his deer like a man
and a pot-hunter. And not that alone. He
still further distinguished himself by upsetting
the canoe in the excitement and exultation of
the moment, by which feat he not only succeeded in giving us both a good ducking, but in
losing his rifle and extinguishing the lamp,
which, as our matches were wet, we had not the
means of relighting. He got his deer, however,
and was supremely happy.

At our shanty on Nameless Lake, as, indeed,

at all backwoods camps, the pleasantest hours of the twenty-four were those between supper and turn in. Then every man did his best to come out strong, and even the head guide, who was by nature of a morose and surly disposition, grew cheerful, not to say entertaining. What songs were sung, what stories told, in that tumbledown shanty! how the log walls used to ring with our peals of laughter! A fico for those who would endeavour to persuade men that out of England all is exile, that in the New World the gentleman emigrant will find nothing but hardship and vexation of spirit. We have seen something of life, the pleasures of advanced civilization are not altogether unknown to us, a considerable portion of our existence has been passed in what are generally supposed to be the pleasantest spots on earth, and yet we can truthfully say that the days upon which we look back with the most unalloyed satisfaction are those which we spent in the American backwoods— not in Nova Scotia certainly, but in Canada and the United States.

If the sport in the New York wilderness be not sufficiently good for our settler, he has but to run across Lake Ontario into Canada. He will reach the great Ottawa hunting country in about the same time as he would were his starting-point in Canada West, and the cost of the trip will not be greater. In the fall he will find good duck shooting amongst the Thousand Islands at the head of the St. Lawrence, and if he want salmon fishing, he has only to run down the same river as far as the Saguenay. The distance is considerable, but where there is water communication distance counts for nothing. On board a lake or river steamboat one is almost as comfortable as at an hotel, and the fares are usually extremely moderate. During the summer and autumn months, the north-western New Yorker, like the Canadian, is to a great extent independent of railroads. By the silent highway of the great lakes he can travel north, east, and west, and, should his destination lie south, he can strike the Hudson at Albany, and the Ohio at Pittsburg, a hundred miles or so by rail from Cleveland, on Lake Erie. A pleasanter trip than that up the lakes to the brand new town of Duluth, at the head of Lake Superior, could not be desired. Up Lake Erie to Detroit, through the river St. Clair into Lake Huron, and by the Sault St. Marie into Lake Superior, is, if the weather only be fine, the pleasantest of excursions. Once on Lake Superior, the sportsman has the wilderness before him where to choose. If to escape from the busy haunts of men, and to lose for a season all traces of civilization be his desire, strike in whatever direction he will, he wont be likely to go far astray. All that he has to do is to walk straight ahead; the country seats of the resident gentry and the hotels that he will see on the road between Duluth and the Pacific will not disturb his peace of mind, nor detract from the pleasures of the journey.

In our opinion the pleasantest way of seeing the great lakes is from aboard a small yacht— say, of six or eight tons measurement. Such boats are to be found in most of the lake ports; and if the hirer go properly to work, he will have no difficulty in chartering one at a moderate figure. It wont cost him much to sail her. Presuming he have a friend with him able to lend a helping hand, one experienced lakesman and a loblolly-boy is all the crew that will be necessary. The round trip is a long one—upwards of three thousand miles, if we include Lake Michigan — but although long, it will scarcely be found wearisome. The constant change of scenery as one glides past headland, bay, and islet—the unflagging interest taken by all on board in the yacht's behaviour—the alternations of hope and despondency as the wind freshens or dies away—draws aft or forward—the nightly camp pitchings, for unless the flies are particularly troublesome, it is better to bring up at sunset, and remain ashore until daybreak ; these, and a hundred other little excitements, prevent the miles from appearing long, and the time from hanging heavily. If it should do so, the voyageur has the remedy in his own hands. He has only to put the yacht about, or head her for the nearest lake port having rail communication, and return home by land instead of water.

With a few general observations we can now leave New York State. For the man of independent means it is, to our mind, the most desirable State in the Union—for the needy one the least so. It is not a State where the gentleman emigrant will be likely to grow rich by farming, nor where he can live at his ease on the interest of four or five thousand pounds. If he have no more than that, Canada is in every respect the more desirable country of the two; and unless he have at least ten thousand pounds, he may strike New York out of his list of States to be visited. And the same in a less degree may be said of New Jersey and Pennsylvania. In that they are long-settled States, having good roads, towns, and markets, they are highly desirable abodes—in that land is dear and labour high, they are not.

New Jersey is a most happily situated little State. Possessing good towns of her own, and with the two most populous cities of the Union —New York and Philadelphia—on either side of her, she has many attractions for the man of means; but for him alone. For the *bonâ fide* farmer—he who is altogether dependent on the produce of his land for subsistence—she has but few. A considerable portion of the State is poor and sandy, and the good land is just as dear, if not dearer, than in the adjoining State of New York. When a really desirable estate is advertised for sale, there is always plenty of bidders— New York and Philadelphia merchants in search of a country seat—men to whom a few thousand dollars, more or less, is a matter of indifference. It would never pay to enter into competition with them. It is not the farmers of New Jersey who drive 2-40 nags, and whose balance at the bank is the largest, but the fruit-growers, market-gardeners, and, above all, the manufacturers; for although not a manufacturing State, in the strict sense of the term, New Jersey has many industries—some peculiarly her own— the concoction of "Lightning," and other vile potables to wit. New Jersey is a nice little, tight little State; but unless the emigrant be to a certain extent independent, or unless he go in for fruit-growing, which requires capital, or for market-gardening, which requires experience, or become a manufacturer of cider, apple-jack, peach-brandy, and other Borgian compounds, which requires no other qualification, that we can see, but a total absence of all principle, she is not the State for him ; and he can strike her likewise out of his list.

Pennsylvania cannot be dismissed in the same off-hand way. When writing of a State possessing an area of some fifty thousand square miles, a little more circumspection must be used. New Jersey being a very small State, bearing, as regards size, pretty much the same relation to Pennsylvania that Yorkshire does to the rest of England, to sum up her advantages, disadvantages, and resources, is a comparatively easy matter. Not so those of a State like Pennsylvania. Her vast extent puts any such general summary out of the question. It would never do to assert that in Pennsylvania land is dear, for in some parts it is cheap—that the soil is rich or poor, productive or unproductive, for it varies—that it is an agricultural State, for some districts are mining, others manufacturing—that it is not the State for our gentleman immigrant, for if he search long enough and travel far enough, he will be certain to find a suitable location.

To attempt the description of the entire State from the Delaware to the Ohio, from the Potomac to Lake Erie—to minutely lay down its geographical features, its rivers, mountains, and valleys—to pass in review its resources, agricultural, mineral, and manufacturing—would, even if we possessed the requisite information, which we do not, take up altogether more space than we can spare. It would fill volumes, and we feel confident that there are few Pennsylvanians whose knowledge of their native State is sufficiently extensive to enable them to undertake the task.

Our knowledge of the State is somewhat limited; our "experiences" having been picked up during a two months' residence, three weeks of which were spent in Philadelphia. We cannot, therefore, speak as authoritatively of its merits and demerits as we did when describing those of New York, where we passed as many years. The most that we can do is to give our reasons for having recommended it to the favourable notice of the emigrant, and they are these—

In the first place, Philadelphia, its capital, is to our mind one of the pleasantest cities in the United States. It may not be as fashionable as New York, nor as "elegant" as Boston, nor as "monumental" as Baltimore, nor as "go-a-

head" as Chicago; but it is a clean, well-built
city, possessing many handsome public buildings,
and one of the best, if not the very best market in North America. Although the "city of
Penn the apostle"—the "Quaker City"—there
is nothing Quakerish about the inhabitants.
They are just as gay and as sociable as other
Americans, and rather more affable to foreigners
than the New Yorkers, who, although very hospitable and obliging to those who come with
proper letters of introduction, or have handles
to their names, or who possess an European
reputation, are by no means so ready to put
themselves out of the way for the stranger
whose advent has not been duly heralded. An
Englishman would experience no difficulty in
gaining admittance to the best circles, unless,
indeed, he thought proper to retain his insular
frigidity of manner, or, worse still, attempted
to lay down the law to the natives. And not
in Philadelphia only, in every part of the State
that we visited we found the people friendly
and obliging. We have heard that in the mining districts, as in our "Black Country," the
inhabitants are rough and churlish; but unless
our immigrant invested his capital in some iron,
coal, or oil company, he would scarcely select
Pittsburg or Petrolia as his place of residence.

His home would be on the banks of the Delaware above Philadelphia—near Harrisburg on the Susquehanna—or a little to the northward of the Virginia boundary line, in the vicinity of Frostburg or Gettysburg.

Another reason for our placing Pennsylvania far before every Western State is, that it does not come under the denomination of "a poor man's paradise." Not having been bepuffed and belauded by a lot of land speculators and railway agents, it has hitherto escaped what may be called emigration inundation. We have no statistics to refer to, but we think we may safely say that the native population is at least quadruple the foreign, and that of the aliens the Germans are in a blessed majority, and no slight blessing either, as those who know the "Free West" can testify.

Our third and last reason is, that just as certain counties in England are "home" counties, so is Pennsylvania a "home" State. It lies adjacent to the Empire City—New York. Its western boundary is certainly three hundred miles distant, but what is three hundred miles in a country where miles are calculated by the thousand, and where men speak of running across to San Francisco as unconcernedly as we do of running over to Ireland, or down to

Edinburgh, by the "Wild Irish" or "Flying Scotch" mails? Even though he have no intention of returning, it is a great consolation to the exile to be able to think, as he looks seawards, "Old England lies just over there across the water; in ten days I could be there." We presume it to be consolatory from our own feelings, which we can well remember. How often, when travelling in the Australian bush, and in other remote places, have we asked ourselves the question, "What compensation would induce you to spend the best years of your life in this howling wilderness?" and the answer was invariably the same— "No compensation whatsoever." And so it would be to-day. Place us at a reasonable distance from civilization—let us only feel that we are not altogether cut off from the world, and though all the marvels of the age we live in were to be seen gratis just round the corner, the chances are that we would not take the trouble to go even that far to look at them. Tell us that they are at a distance of thirteen thousand, or even three thousand miles, and that, travel as we may, some weeks must elapse before we can see them, and we want to be off at once. And so it is, we opine, with most men—it is human nature.

The principal objections to the State of Pennsylvania are, so far as we can judge—firstly, the

price of land. Although in the remoter districts
land can be purchased at a low figure, in the
picked spots it is decidedly dear; almost as dear
as in the State of New York—double and treble
what it is in Virginia. Good land in choice localities
sells as high as 40*l.* an acre; and to make a living
out of it at that price, the farmer must be other
than an amateur. Then labour is dear. According
to the latest quotations the weekly wages of farm
labourers is 2*l.* 8*s.*—nearly double the Canadian
average—and with hands at that hire it would
never answer for the farmer to go gadding about
the country, leaving his farm to take care of itself.
He would have to stick to his acres, and look
well after his helps; for, like Paddy, Jonathan
has a remarkable aptitude for "putting in the
time" whenever the chance is given him. That
flour, meat, and provisions of every description
are dearer in Pennsylvania than in Canada and
the Western States, is all in the farmer's favour.
To the non-farmer, however—to the man whose
sole object in emigrating is to live on the interest
of his capital, and to make the most of it—the
prevailing high prices is a very serious objection.
For him Canada is out and out the more desirable residence, more especially if he be fond of
sport. If Pennsylvania be not a poor man's
paradise, neither is it the paradise of sportsmen.

Fair deer shooting may be had in the vicinity of the Alleghanies and on the beech-ridges; and in the season there are plenty of duck on the waters of Chesapeake Bay, which, although not strictly in the State, is but a short distance from the boundary line. But that is about all. Reed-bird shooting is considered fine sport by the Philadelphians; but the man who objects to being peppered, and who has a due regard for his eyesight, will decline all invitations to join in the fun. To stand in momentary expectation of receiving a charge of shot in one's person as one is poled through the high reeds on the river-bank may be very exciting, but it can hardly be called sport.

We now come to the last State on our list— Virginia; for what we have just said of Pennsylvania applies in a great measure to Ohio, whilst what we are about to say of Virginia will apply in like manner to Maryland. If Pennsylvania be deemed unsuitable by the intending emigrant, he may dismiss Ohio from his thoughts; if Virginia do not come up to his ideal, neither will little Maryland. In no respect that we can see is Ohio superior to Pennsylvania as a field for the gentleman emigrant. Neither is the climate more healthy, nor is the soil more productive, nor are the people more friendly—quite the reverse. Land may be

a trifle cheaper; but as the distance to New York
and the seaboard is greater, gain there is none.
For our own part we infinitely prefer Philadelphia
to Cincinnati—Harrisburg to Columbus—and
were we to settle in the State it would not be on
the banks of the Ohio river, but somewhere near
Cleveland on Lake Erie. The much-vaunted
" Beautiful River" is no more to be compared to
the Hudson than is her Catawba wine to Clicquot.

Land and labour are considerably higher in
Maryland than in Virginia; but then the former
State remained, or was forced to remain, neutral
during the Civil War, and escaped scot free, or
nearly so. The manumission of the slaves was
in her case a gain rather than a loss.

It is not without a certain hesitation that we
now proceed to lay before the reader our reasons
for giving Virginia so high a place in the list of
States, and for asserting that, as a home for the
emigrant of moderate means, she is second to
none; for we feel that, strive as we may, we can
hardly write as impartially as we ought to do.
Hitherto we have had no particularly strong
feelings one way or the other, and have written
without fear, favour, or affection. In a general
way we may have expressed our likes and dis-
likes—and we do not see how we could well have
done otherwise—but whether the reader went to

Maine or Texas, to New York or California, was
to us a matter of perfect indifference. But it is
not so with Virginia. We candidly admit that
we have strong Virginian " proclivities;" and
that if we can in any legitimate way aid the
inhabitants of the Old Dominion in their endeavour to induce English gentlemen to settle
amongst them, we shall do so. We shall not
attempt to prove, à la handbook compiler, that
Virginia is the most healthful, the most fertile,
the most beautiful, the most " Paradisiacal"
country on the face of the earth, for she needs no
such trumpeting; but simply that she is a good
country—a very good country—for the gentleman
emigrant whose capital is insufficient to start him
as a sheep-farmer in Australia, and yet who is
not so poor that he must content himself with a
half-cleared farm in some Western State or
Canadian back settlement. More—that when all
has been said in favour of Canada that can be said,
it will be found that in many respects Virginia is
the more desirable residence of the two.

Prior to the Civil War, Virginia was, of all
places in the world, the very last to which we
should have advised the needy gentleman to
emigrate. Society was divided into four classes,
the planter, the trader, the mean-white, and the
slave ; and the settler who had not the money to

purchase a plantation, and negroes to work it, was relegated to class number three. He was a " mean"—*i.e.*, a poor white man, ranking above the negro, but who nevertheless despised him for his poverty, just as in other lands, England for example, menials turn up their noses at tutors, governesses, and poor folk generally, because of their poverty. This was more especially the case in Eastern Virginia, where the plantations were larger, the planters wealthier, and the negroes more numerous than in the western section of the State. In "Ole Varginny" the mean-white was considered very mean indeed, and in nine cases out of ten justly so, for a lazier, surlier, more ignorant being was not to be found in North America.

But for the man who was not poor, or who, if poor, was not obliged to expose his poverty, Virginia was a very pleasant land. The planters were a genial, easy-going, indolent race, and hospitable to a fault. They kept open house, and unless the visitor attacked the " institution," he could hardly outstay his welcome. The only difficulty lay in getting away at all. Everything that could be done to make his stay agreeable was done, and if he did not enjoy himself it was his own fault, and not that of his host. Fonder of dogs, horses, and field sports than of dollars, cents, and commercial pursuits, the Virginian planter had much more of the English squire about him than of the Yankee farmer. Perhaps we ought rather to say of the Irish squire, for he not only lived up to his income, but beyond it, and was as improvident as improvident could be. "Sufficient unto the day" was his motto, and when he ran short of money, which was not unfrequently, he raised what he wanted by a mortgage on his estate. If it was not paid off next year it would the next, or the next, or in that good time a-coming when, there being no more abolitionists, underground railways, or governmental interference in the rights of slaveowners, a remunerative price could be obtained for the "commodity." And so he lived on the fat of the land, and hunted, and played "poker," and made trips to Europe and to New York, and disported himself at fashionable watering-places, and enjoyed himself in his own thriftless fashion until the outbreak of the Civil War. The boom of the first gun fired on Fort Sumter roused him from his lethargy, and he became forthwith an altered man. . We were in Virginia during the first months of the war, and witnessed the metamorphosis, and a wonderful one it was. Had we not seen it with our own eyes, we could never have believed that in so short a time so great a change was possible; for the smoke of that first gun had scarcely cleared away ere the Sybarites of 1860 had become the hardy soldiers of 1861. How bravely they fought, how, ever foremost in the fray, they time after time hurled back the invaders, and how, men and supplies alike exhausted, they were at length forced to yield, let impartial history tell.

When Lee surrendered, the planters returned to their homes ruined men, and the Virginians the most hopelessly ruined of all. Virginia had been the chief battle-ground, and desolation marked the track of the invader. All along the different roads " To Richmond"—and very hard roads to travel the Federals found them—farms and plantations had been so often and so effectually " requisitioned," that on their return the rightful owners found little of which to take repossession save weed-choked fields and gutted homesteads. Differently circumstanced to their brother planters in the more southern States, they could not set to work to repair damages, for the damage done was irreparable. Unfortunately for them, theirs had been an essentially " slave raising" State—their wealth had lain more in the labourer than in the land: to them emancipation was only another word for ruination. They could not pick up the shoved

and the hoe that Sambo had thrown down, and
take his place in the tobacco field, for they were
physically unfitted for the task; they could not
hire labour, for they had no money; they could
not sell their estates, for no one wanted to purchase. Things were at a deadlock. Their one
chance lay in being able to induce men of small
capital to settle amongst them. If they could
sell some portion of their estates, say one half,
or a third, they might be able to raise sufficient
money to pay off the mortgages, and bring the
remainder under cultivation. But where to find
these men of small capital? That was the question. Not in the Northern States, for they
loathed the very name of Yankee. Not in the
Canadas, for the Canadians had already more
land than they knew what to do with, and were
much more disposed to borrow than to invest.
Not amongst the newly arrived Irish and German
emigrants at Castle Garden and other depôts, for
their only capital was bone and sinew. If the
men they wanted were to be found at all, they
must be looked for in England. And so advertisements, addressed to England's younger son-
dom, to retired officers of both services, and to
small capitalists generally, were inserted in the
leading papers, and letters were written and
pamphlets published laudatory of Virginia, the

"Old Dominion." Compared with similar productions, they were, as a rule, extremely moderate in tone. Virginia's claim to favourable notice was based on her being able to offer cheap land and labour, a mild climate, good roads, and accessible markets, and last, not least, the assurance of a cordial welcome.

Let us carefully consider these several advantages, and endeavour to determine whether they exist in fact or only in the imagination of the writers.

"Cheap land!" Virginia is not the only county that holds out that tempting bait to the emigrant. Cheap land is the watchword of every land-jobber and emigration agent whose advertisements appear in the papers. "A free grant of a hundred acres!" "20*l.* land-order warrants per adult, issued to persons paying their own full passage!" "Land allotments from 40 to 320 acres, by paying a deposit of twenty-five per cent. at the rate of 1*l.* per acre!" These are the inducements held out to the lacklands, who little dream that land can be too cheap— that it can be dear even at a gift; and yet it is so. Land may be dear at fifty cents—cheap at fifty pounds the acre, and to decide whether it be cheap or dear without having seen it is utterly impossible. Descriptive particulars count for

nothing. A farm may be first-class in all respects save one, and that one deficiency may
render it comparatively valueless. *Caveat emptor.*
It is not the vendor who has to point out the de-
fects, but the purchaser who has to discover
them, and the man who would purchase a farm
by telegraph, like " Caribou's Friend," would invest his capital in a Californian diamond mine,
with no better security than the verbal guarantee
of the owner. Not until the would-be purchaser
has carefully inspected the property—not until
he has resided six months, and a year would be
better, in its vicinity—ought he to lay out a sixpence; for the bargain once concluded, it will be
too late to say *if* I had only known this, that, or
the other—*if* I had only waited, what disappointment and expense I might have avoided."
When writing of Canada, we strongly advised
the intending emigrant to take his time in the
purchase of a farm—to think twice before making
a bid—to acquaint himself with the people before
finally determining to settle amongst them, and
we do so again, now that we are treating of Virginia. The Old Dominion is not Old England,
and instead of there being ten bidders for every
farm, there are ten farms for every bidder. The
new-comer need not be afraid that he will miss
his chance—that if he hesitates some one else

will be beforehand with him—he may rest assured that he will lose nothing by waiting. If he
do not get this farm he will that, and the chances
are that the last he hears of will suit him best.

Virginia being a very large State, having
great diversity of soil and climate, to deal with it
in its entirety would be mere waste of time.
That the reader may have some idea of its
general characteristics and resources, it must be
divided, according to its geographical configura-
tions, into regions. It will be sufficient for our
purpose if we divide it into four—Eastern
Virginia, Old Virginia, the Valley lands, and
Western Virginia; for the "Panhandle," that
narrow strip of country lying between the Ohio
river and the Pennsylvania border line, may be
said, like the district of Columbia, to belong to
itself, and be passed over accordingly.

Eastern Virginia, or what we choose to desig-
nate Eastern Virginia, is that portion of the
State stretching from the longitude of Richmond to
the sea. Although some of the best land is to
be found there, it is not the district that we
should select as a residence, for the climate
leaves much to be desired. Its unhealthiness
has, we think, been rather over estimated by the
letter-writers and pamphleteers, who hail mostly
from the Piedmont district; but there is no

denying that along the shores of Chesapeake
Bay, and the rivers flowing into it, fever is very
prevalent. That it would be little short of mad-
ness for any man with a wife and family to
settle in a malarious district, no one but a land-
jobber would attempt to disprove. But then
every man is not blessed with a wife and family,
and the single man, who is not afraid of fever,
who has no one's health but his own to consider,
and whose object is to make money, might, in
our opinion, go further and fare worse.

Eastern Virginia is rapidly becoming the
market garden of the Northern States, and New
York and Boston are mainly dependent upon her
for their supply of early vegetables. The demand for this description of southern produce is
daily increasing, and trade is once again beginning to "look up" along the Rappahannock, the
York, and the James—"upper" than in any
other section of the State—the vaunted Piedmont
district not excepted. Market gardening is a
much more profitable business than farming, and
if the emigrant wants to make money "right
smart," Eastern Virginia is the place for him.
We don't advise him to go there—he is his
own master to go where he pleases. We only
tell him that, fever or no fever, Eastern Virginia is the most money-making section of the
State.

Besides, it is not all malarious. The country about Fredericksburg, Richmond, and Petersburg is healthy enough, and if he take time to look about him, there is no reason why he should not be able to find some spot sufficiently distant from the coast to be healthy, and yet near enough to make market gardening a profitable undertaking. Want of experience need not deter him from making the attempt. In the Sunny South nature does her own forcing, and a very small knowledge of horticulture suffices to grow peas, cucumbers, and tomatoes. Several inexperienced Englishmen have already gone into the business, and are by all accounts doing well, and it would be surprising if they did otherwise. If with cheap land and labour, a season six weeks in advance of that of the Northern States, and water communication at his door, the market gardener of Eastern Virginia cannot manage to make his business pay, and handsomely, there must be a screw loose somewhere.

We confine our observations to market gardening, for the country offers no special advantages to the ordinary farmer. District No. 2—Old Virginia—that section of the State lying between Richmond and the Blue Mountain Range, is better adapted to the growth of wheat and hay, and what to many is a matter of even greater importance, the climate is much the healthier of

the two.   Taking it all in all, it is, we think, the
one which would be most likely to suit the small
capitalist, especially if he be a married man.   The
soil is not so rich as in the Shenandoah valley,
but the price of land is considerably lower—
absurdly cheap when compared with the prices
ruling in the adjoining States of Maryland and
Pennsylvania.   At the present time good farms
can be purchased for 6*l.* or 7*l.* per acre, buildings
thrown in, and when these buildings are of brick
or stone, and in fair repair, the actual cost of the
land may be safely set down at 40 or 50 per cent.
below that quotation.   We have been assured that
in several instances the price paid was less than
the original cost of the buildings, but our informant
was not prepared to assert that the purchaser
had the best of the bargain.   For our own part
we have no faith in these "awful sacrifices," for
they are, so far. as our experience goes, nothing
else but awful swindles.

In Old Virginia especially, great caution is
necessary in the purchase of land, for much of it
is worn out, and for the present valueless.   That
there should be any good land at all is surprising,
for tobacco is a very exhausting crop; tobacco
was the staple of the country, and the Virginian
planters were, without exception, the worst
farmers in existence.   Having generally plenty

of unreclaimed land upon which to fall back,
they seldom troubled themselves to keep the cultivated portion of their estates up to the mark,
and in a productive condition. They got what
they could out of a field, and when it was thoroughly worn out, and would yield no more,
they broke up some fresh land in its place. In
land, as in most other things, there are, of course,
different degrees of badness. Some of it is so
completely exhausted that it would cost more
than its worth to restore it to anything approaching its former fertility; but a considerable portion might, under judicious management, be
reclaimed at a comparatively small outlay. The
investor must use his own judgment in that
matter. Only let him not be too particular. In
avoiding Scylla, he may fall into Charybdis; by
keeping clear of poor land, he may steer into the
Court of Bankruptcy. Even in poor beggared
Virginia, for very superior farms, comparatively
high prices are asked and given, and the model
farmer may pay too dear for his hobby. As we
have more than once endeavoured to impress on
the reader, it is not the farm that costs the most
that invariably pays the best, and in the purchase
of one the investor ought above all things to
keep well within his means. Far better a second-
class farm and plenty of capital to work it, than

a fancy one with creditors continually hammering at the door. Keep well within your means is a piece of advice that we can offer without any proviso or reservation whatsoever, for it applies to all alike, to the poor man as well as to the rich, to the practical farmer as well as to the amateur. But that said, we are at the end of our Latin. Until we know our man, we cannot advise him as to the description of farm he ought to select, nor state the price he could afford to pay for it. As a general rule, however, the better the farmer the poorer the land he can afford to take up, for the same farm that would pay, and pay well, in the hands of the practical agriculturist, might very probably ruin the amateur. The former has a double pull over the latter, in that he is both farmer and valuator. Knowing his business, his bid is based, not on the appraised, but on the real value of the land; and when it comes into his possession he is able to work it to the best advantage. In his case the risk is reduced to a minimum. Presuming that he really is a practical farmer, and not a mere theorist, he will be able to determine approximately how much it will cost per acre to put the land into fair average condition, and that once done the rest is merely a question of dollars and cents. If the amount saved on the purchase-money—say 4*l.* per acre—be insufficient for the purpose, the investment is a bad one; if just enough, a fair one; if more than enough, a good one. *Q. e. d.*

The calculations of the amateur being at the best mere guesswork, he should avoid all investments of a speculative nature, and not allow himself to be tempted into the purchase of poor land merely because it is cheap. Let him leave the impoverished land to those who know how to doctor it, and by paying a little more secure a farm that is in a fairly productive condition. There are plenty of such farms to be found in Old Virginia, and their price may, as we have already stated, be set down at 6*l.* or 7*l.* per acre, buildings thrown in. That last is a very important consideration. Building is costly in Virginia, and the man who dabbles in bricks and mortar will probably live to rue it. Better medium land and good buildings upon it than virgin soil and no homestead. Even supposing that he paid 10*l.*, or even 12*l.* an acre—a very exceptional price indeed—what is 12*l.* an acre for a good farm with substantial stone house and outbuildings? He would have to give considerably more in Canada, and double or treble that amount in the adjoining States of Pennsylvania, Ohio, and Maryland. That it can long remain at its present price is morally impossible. It must rise, but whether the rise will be slow or rapid no man living can tell. Much depends on the Virginians themselves. Their outspoken abhorrence of everything Yankee has hitherto deterred Northern farmers from settling in the country, and until the bitter feelings created by the late war shall have passed away they will continue to fight shy of the Old Dominion. Before the reaction takes place is the time to purchase, and as it is impossible to say how soon it will come, that time is now. Come when it may land will never be cheaper than it is at the present moment, and money judiciously invested therein at ruling prices is as safe as if it were invested in Government stock. More profitable investments there are, no doubt, but they are not open to every one. The Western land-jobber would turn up his nose at any speculation that did not promise to return him at least cent. per cent. in two or three years' time. But the Western land-jobber is one individual and the gentleman emigrant is another. The former knows the ropes—he is hand-and-glove with every railway promoter, "lobby-man," and "carpet-bagger" in Washington—and when there is a "good thing" in perspective, he gets timely notice, and is one of the first to cut in. He cuts boldly—goes the " whole hog or none." If the good thing prove to be really a good thing he makes his pile and is jubilant. If it do not, he anathematizes his luck and pays up, or " busts up," as the case may be — most probably the latter.

It is very different with the latter gentleman. He has no lobby-man at his elbow to put him up to good things, and if he want a friendly hint he must pay for it. He likewise labours under the disadvantage of being a benighted Britisher. He is not smart in the American sense of the term, and to enter into successful competition with some of the very smartest men of the most enlightened country in creation, smartness is a desideratum. We do not say that it is indispensable. Speculation is speculation, and whether one's capital be invested in land, mines, or Government securities, much depends on luck. The prizes are not always drawn by the clever ones, but for all that they generally manage to get the lion's share, especially " Out West." Fortune might favour the bold Briton ; he might make a lucky hit and clear three or four hundred per cent. on his investment, but he might not. An alien, an interloper, a nobody without *locus standi* or interest at court, he could hardly expect to divide the spoil with the personal friends of Presidents, Ministers, Members of Congress, and Railway Kings. He would have to content himself with whatever pickings these Republican Magnificos chose to leave him, and as they generally cut pretty close to the bone, the said pickings would not be likely to cause plethora. He would get his twenty or five-and-twenty per cent., and he could do the same with less trouble in Virginia.

There the market is an open one. In order to get his money on, it is not necessary that the speculator should have the protection of Mr. Senator This or Mr. Director That. There is no favouritism, and the newly arrived emigrant can purchase on the same terms as the Member of Congress. If the property is in the Encumbered Estates Court, or the Court which in the Old Dominion does duty for that Hibernian institution, he can either make an offer to the Commissioners or wait until it is put up at auction. If in the hands of the owner, he has only to pursue the same tactics as are recommended to the Canada-bound emigrant in our opening chapters; for if not quite so almighty smart at a trade as the Yankee, the Virginian is more than a match for the average Englishman. The golden rule in dealing with an American, be he Canadian, Yankee, or Virginian, is "never to want anything 'real bad.' " In other words, always try to appear as indifferent as possible; for the less you seem disposed to buy the more eager the owner will be to sell, and the lower the value he will set upon his commodity.

Although 300*l*. has been given as the minimum amount of capital required by those who would settle in Virginia, we should be very sorry to advise any man to go there who has not more than that at command. Virginia is not a poor man's paradise; and if 300*l*., or even 500*l*., be the sum total of his capital, he would be much more likely to succeed in Canada or the Free West. It is all very well to put down land so much—house so much—stock so much—total so much—these items form but a portion of the settler's disbursements; and the gentlemen who calculate in this off-hand way are very untrustworthy authorities. Every man who is at all conversant with the subject, knows that it is not so much the large payments as the small ones which run away with the emigrant's money; and to lump them together under the heading of incidental expenses is unpardonable. " Incidentals, say 30*l*. !" Thirty humbugs! If the incidental expenses of the three hundred pounder don't swallow up a good third of his capital he is a lucky man.

Our minimum is fifteen hundred pounds, and even then one would have to sail very close to the wind. With double that amount the emigrant might be certain of doing well. He could purchase a farm of two hundred or two hundred and fifty acres, and have sufficient left to stock it properly, and to meet all incidental expenses without running into debt. Properly managed, a two hundred acre farm ought to support him well; more than that no small farmer has any right to expect, whether the scene of his labours be Virginia, Canada, or the Antipodes. The Virginian farmer is no more likely to become a millionaire than is his brother of Ontario, New York, Iowa, or Victoria, but he enjoys several advantages which these gentlemen do not. In that the climate is milder, he is better off than the Canadian; in that land and labour are cheaper, than the farmer of the Middle States; in that the country is longer-settled, the roads better, and the markets nearer than the Westerner, in that he is not at the ends of the earth, than the Australian.

It is not without reason that the Virginian asserts that, taking it all in all, his native State offers more solid advantages to the English gentleman of moderate capital than any other emigration field in the world. The Govern-

ment may be better, and the taxes lighter in
Canada—land cheaper and crops heavier in the
Western States—the Australian climate be
slightly the better of the two—but, taking one
thing with another, Virginia has the pull over
them all. In no other country are so many advantages to be found combined—mild climate, cheap
land and labour, ready-made farms, good roads,
schools, and markets, and all within twelve days'
sail of England. The chief drawbacks are that
it is a conquered and impoverished country, and
that there is still a considerable negro population.
But then if the country were not impoverished,
land would be dearer; if there were no negroes,
labour would be higher. It is not the alien, the
new-arrival, who has reason to grumble at the
present state of things; but the native Virginian
—the poor ruined owner of the soil, who can
remember when the Old Dominion stood
first on the list of States; and when, in the
words of Randolphe of Roanoake, she "grew
presidents." Under no circumstances can it be
pleasant to live in a conquered country; for
unless a man have a heart of stone, he must sym-
pathize with the people amongst whom his lot
has been cast, and resent the indignities heaped
upon them by the victors. But unpleasant is
one thing, unendurable another; and since the

termination of the war, life to the Virginians has been nearly so. They may not have been so cruelly persecuted as the South Carolinians; but they have been made to " toe the line"—to understand the full significance of the words *Væ victis !* Poor Alsace-Lorraine! Poor Secessia! rather. German rule in the annexed provinces has been mild and beneficent when compared with that of the Northerners in the rebellious States. In Strasburg and Metz are soldiers and officials galore, but, blessed immunity! there are no carpet-baggers.

The same argument holds good in respect to the second disadvantage—the presence of a free negro population. Sambo's room is always more desirable than his company, but he is not half so objectionable to the Englishman as to the American. The former never having known him as other than a free man, can live with him on terms of equality without much loss of caste. The latter cannot. It is impossible for him to forget that the coloured gentleman, who goes swaggering past as if the whole place belonged to him, who lays down the law and sits in judgment, was once his slave, his chattel, and the very sight of him is poison. To the one he is simply objectionable, to the other a never-ending source of torment and mortification.

But these two evils will not be everlasting.
Time, the great consoler, will heal the first—the
migration of the negroes southwards the second.
President Grant has already expressed his opinion
that the time has arrived for the men in possession — the carpet-baggers — to "unload," and
with the departure of these Yankee bumbailiffs
much of the present bitterness of spirit will pass
away. Mild as is the climate, it is not sufficiently so for the sun-loving Ethiopian, and he
will be "off for Charleston," or some warmer
latitude, whenever he can raise the money to pay
his way. When the black man walks out the
white labourer will walk in, and his advent will
mark a new and brighter era in Virginian history; for whether the Old Dominion regain her
former place in the roll of states, or whether she
do not, whether she continue to grow presidents
and to have it all her own way in Congress, or
whether she have to play second fiddle, she will
have gained far more than she has lost, in that
she has been freed from the incubus, from the
curse of slavery. If she lose in political power,
she will gain in material wealth. Slave labour
is the costliest of all, and under the old régime
she could not compete as a producing State with
her free neighbours. Now she can; and with
her immense resources, mineral as well as agri-

cultural, there is no reason why she should not
ere long rival Ohio in her yield of wheat, and
Pennsylvania in her yearly output of coal and
iron.   There is a great future in store for
Virginia, if her sons only put their shoulders to
the wheel, and make the most of their oppor-
tunities ; and they will do so, for the " grit" is
there.

But they want assistance, monetary as well as
muscular, and they therefore invite Englishmen
of a certain class—the very men to whom this
work is addressed—to come and help them. And
they might do worse than accept the invitation ;
we cannot see, indeed, how they can do better.
Canada is a good, a very good country, for the
gentleman emigrant—that we have admitted
over and over again—but were Virginia in a
slightly more settled state, the negroes not
quite so numerous as at present, and we on the
look out for a home beyond the sea, it is more
than probable that we should decide in favour of
the Old Dominion.   Did the choice lie between
Virginia and some other State or territory of the
American Union, we should not hesitate for an
instant, unless, indeed, we had a handsome
independence, and then we should probably select
New York.

It is no slight advantage to live amongst a

friendly people, which the Virginians decidedly
are. The inhabitants of the Northern, Middle,
and Western States, if not exactly hostile to
England and the English, are very far from
being as friendly disposed as some well-intentioned gentlemen would have us believe them
to be. We speak of the masses. What the
Hon. William Ewarts, Dr. John Draper, or the
President of the Cornell University may have
said amounts to very little. They spoke for
themselves and their colleagues, a select body of
intelligent and liberally minded men, not in the
name of the American people. That "there is
a generous and perfect sympathy between the
educated men of England and the educated men
of the United States," we are perfectly aware. So
there is, notwithstanding recent occurrences,
between those of France and Germany. Men
who have received a liberal education have generally liberal ideas, and "the small matters of
difference and political interests which divide
country from country" do not influence them.
But, in the United States, what proportion do
the enlightened and liberally minded bear to the
ignorant and the prejudiced? We should be
sorry to guess. The schoolmaster may be ubi-
quitous in the wide domains of Uncle Samuel,
but men may know how to read, write, and

cypher, and yet be as illiberal and narrow-minded as so many Chinese.

That the fierce hatred of the Celt for the Saxon has not cooled in crossing the Atlantic, the late Fenian raids and demonstrations sufficiently prove. It is certainly not the Irish who are friendly disposed towards us, and they form no inconsiderable portion of the entire community. Neither is it the German element. Hans divides the English-speaking race into two bodies, the American and the Irish. Those who are not American are Irish, and the English not being Americans, are naturally Irish too. That the Germans hate the Irish, no American will, we think, deny, and hating Paddy, how can they love John Bull? It is certainly not amongst the alien population that our admirers and well-wishers are to be found; and if the natives, the pure-blooded Americans, are friendly disposed towards us, it must be admitted that they show their friendship in a very strange way. Except on one memorable occasion, when an American Commodore took upon himself the responsibility of lending us assistance, we cannot call to mind a single instance where " Brother Jonathan" has remembered that " blood is thicker than water." In every " difficulty" that has arisen—" The Boundary Difficulty," " The Right of Search

Difficulty," "The San Juan Difficulty," "The Fisheries · Difficulty," "The Alabama Difficulty," the young gentleman has ever been more disposed to fight than to arrange, and if he have come to terms, it is simply because the terms were all in his favour.

Professor Tyndall asserts that during his four months' residence in the United States he did not hear a single whisper hostile to England. He was singularly fortunate. Our experience has been precisely the reverse. Northwards of the Potomac we have seldom heard a word said in her favour. The political orator on the stump, the lawyer addressing the jury, the newspaper editor from his editorial chair, one and all had their slap at GREAT Britain. In the United States, where every man is a born politician, the best card in the national game of Brag is the one on which is depicted the American Eagle screeching and flapping his wings over the defunct British Lion.

But a distinction must be made between the politician and the man. As we have already had occasion to remark—Jonathan before the public is one individual, Jonathan in private another; and the same man who has been abusing England in the most venomous manner the entire morning, will very probably have an English-

man to dine with him in the evening, and be as
amiable to him as mortal man can be.

The more we see of the American people the
less we are able to comprehend them. The
national feeling is ever changing. Like the
mercury in a thermometer—now it is at fever
heat, now at zero. And it is the same with individuals. The man who is all smiles in the morning, may be as surly as a bear with a sore ear in
the afternoon. Your friend to-day may be your
bitterest enemy to-morrow.

In the event of another "difficulty" arising,
those "old cords which unite the hearts of the
two great English-speaking nations," are very
likely to snap ; and as such a catastrophe is by
no means improbable, we should, all things considered, prefer having our habitation on the
Southern side of the Potomac, and in the friendly
State of Virginia.

Besides the advantages already enumerated,
there is yet another which most Englishmen
will not fail to appreciate. There is plenty of
sport to be had—duck on Chesapeake Bay, quail
in the fields, ruffed grouse and wild-turkey in the
woods, and capital deer shooting everywhere,
more especially in Western Virginia, and if the
reader settle in the neighbourhood of Charlottes-
ville he will have fox hunting to boot, a pack

of hounds having, it would appear, been recently imported. If that doesn't make his mouth water we don't know what will—why, he wouldn't have better sport in Canada.

But whether his home be in the Piedmont district, or in Eastern Virginia, or in the valley of Shenandoah—we say nothing of Western Virginia, it being still in a primeval state—we feel convinced that he will not repent him of having settled in the Old Dominion. There are many good countries under the sun, but none better than Virginia, and with that assurance we take our leave of him and of America.

AND presuming that you don't succeed in passing your examination—that you are plucked—what then?"

"Oh! in that case I shall emigrate."

"Where?"

"To Australia. Lots of money to be made by sheep farming; or if sheep farming doesn't suit my taste, I can turn sugar or cotton planter."

"And your capital?"

"A thousand."

"Not sufficient."

"Not sufficient! That's all you know about it. Seven hundred and fifty is ample to start a man in the squatting line, and with a couple of hundred pounds or so he can commence cotton or cane planting. There it is in black and white. I suppose you will allow that Mr. What's-his-name is as good an authority on the subject as yourself."

The above is the substance of a conversation which took place not very long since between ourselves on the one part and a young gentleman who was supposed to be studying for the Indian

Civil Service examination on the other. Unless there should happen to turn up a combination of chances in his favour, plucked he would be to a certainty, and of that no man was more fully aware than himself. But he wasn't in the least dispirited, for " if the worst came to the worst he could emigrate."

How many hundreds of well-educated young men are there at the present moment shepherding, hut-keeping, bullock-driving, in one or other of our Australian colonies, who might justly attribute their misfortunes to having read in an evil hour some lying colonial hand-book? We do not speak of the drunken and lazy, who would have come to grief in whatever land their lot might have been cast; but of the sober, hard-working, and well-intentioned, whose mischances have been altogether owing to circumstances beyond their own control. Not only hundreds, but thousands; we have met scores of them ourselves.

Who is this that we see seated under a gum-tree wearily watching the movements of a flock of sheep? The brother of an English squire, whose income is upwards of six thousand per annum.

There ! We have in our mind's eye the whole scene again before us—the cloudless sky over head,

the scanty-foliaged gum trees, the burnt-up
pasturage, the widely extended crescent of white-
fleeced sheep, and seated beside us the shepherd
of the flock. Prithee, gentle shepherd, recount
the story of thy woes. Why not thine as well
as those of any other hapless gentleman emigrant?
One has but to shut one's eyes to change the
venue to the distant American continent, for
whether thy lot be cast in the Australian bush
or amidst the rugged peaks of the Rocky Mountains, it is generally the same old, old story.

"You wish to know how it has come about
that I, a gentleman by birth and education, and
who only four short years ago landed in Melbourne with twelve hundred pounds in my
pocket, am reduced to the sorry plight in which
you see me? It wont take me long to tell you.
It is because I was so stupid as to believe that a
thousand pounds was sufficient capital to commence sheep farming, and that because I was
strong and active, and could shoot, ride, and row,
I was just the sort of man for the colonies.

"When, shortly after my father's death, my elder
brother handed me a cheque for twelve hundred
pounds, quietly hinting as he did so that it was
high time that I should find a home of my own
and some means of subsistence other than spong-
ing upon him, I took the money without a

murmur. Considering the style in which I had been brought up, and the very handsome fortune inherited by the said elder brother, I could not help thinking that he might have added something on his own account; but I said nothing, inwardly determining to show him and my other relatives that I could do without their assistance, and was perfectly competent to make my own way in life. Being convinced that my capital was altogether too small to start me in a respectable line of business in England, I determined to emigrate, and, after considerable deliberation and careful perusal of every hand-book to emigration upon which I could lay hands, I selected Victoria as the land of my future labours. In less than a fortnight after this determination was arrived at I was in Liverpool, and finding the *Great Britain* on the berth, I took a cabin passage aboard her. That is the greatest piece of imprudence of which I can be accused—having gone first-class by steamer instead of intermediate or steerage by sailing ship, and a great act of folly I acknowledge it to have been. On the voyage out I was thrown into the society of men who, in comparison to myself, were veritable millionaires—wealthy squatters, Melbourne and Sydney brokers, and such like. They drank their claret and champagne as a matter of course, insisting on my joining them, and as I was altogether too proud to drink at their expense without standing treat in return, my wine bill came to considerably more than it ought to have done. But this was not all. As we sat chatting of an evening over the social glass of toddy, it was but natural that I should speak of the old home—of the hunters in its stables, the pheasants in its coverts, the carp in its pools—and I was soon considered not only a great authority upon all sporting matters, but was accredited with the possession of as many thousands as I had hundreds lodged in the Melbourne bank. It was not out of bounce that I spoke of those sports and pastimes in which I had from boyhood participated, it was from mere force of habit that I did so. I had no desire to pass for other than I really was—a very needy young man going out to seek his fortune in the colonies—but I had greatness thrust upon me against my will. That a young man should have horses to ride and gamekeepers to escort him when at home, and yet be hard pressed to pay for his bread, let alone his butter, when away from it, sounds natural enough to English ears; but to those unacquainted with our time-honoured institutions, such a state of things would seem simply incredible. I only saw the mistake I had com-

mitted when it was too late, and that I might not
be looked upon as a rank impostor, I had to be
reticent as to the real state of my finances. I
consoled myself with the reflection that that
bond of good fellowship which unites all classes
on shipboard is severed the instant the vessel
arrives in port—that I should in all probability
never meet my fellow-passengers again, and that
it would be easy to make a fresh start. It was
not so to be. Unfortunately, as it turned out, I
had tried hard to make myself agreeable on the
passage. I had told my best stories, sung my
best songs, had, in fact, earned for myself the
reputation of being such a devilish good fellow
that long before we sighted Port Phillip Heads
I had received half-a-dozen invitations to up-
country runs, where I was to have kangaroo
hunting, cattle mustering, and be thoroughly
initiated into all the mysteries of colonial life.
Prudence whispered to me that it would perhaps
be best to decline; but there were so many plausible reasons for accepting—such as the experience
I should gain, the money that I would be en-
abled to save, and a score of similar ones—that I
hesitated—I hesitated, and, as a natural consequence, ended by accepting. One fine morning
saw me mounted on a serviceable nag, bound to
a friend's station as a visitor—had it been as

factotum at a fixed monthly wage I might
perhaps have a different tale to tell. All went
well at first. Of the kangaroo hunting and
cattle mustering, about which so much had been
said, I certainly saw next to nothing, but there
was plenty of work going on about the head
station, at which a Newchum could lend a hand,
and I was rather pleased that it should be so, for
was I not gaining experience? And so for
six months or more I helped to wash sheep,
to roll fleeces, to brand bales of wool, and to
carry rations, to the entire satisfaction of my
squatter friend, for he was not the man to have
any false delicacy about making a visitor useful.
The time had at length arrived, I thought, when
I might safely sound my host as to the possibility
of my obtaining a small interest in the run, after
the manner suggested by the author of the
'Hand-book to Squatting,' or some such trust-
worthy manual. He had indeed more than once
hinted that he was heavily indebted to some
Melbourne brokers, who had advanced him
money to purchase stock, and that he should like
to shake himself clear of them, could he only
raise the necessary amount, for the interest they
demanded was exorbitant, and sufficient to ruin
any man, no matter how good his run. Here
was the very chance. I could not, of course,

find the money to pay off all his liabilities, but even a thousand pounds would be something towards it. Supposing he was lent, say twelve hundred pounds without interest, would he be willing to give a bill at five years' date for one thousand, and, in lieu of the balance, four hundred two-year-old ewes, with the right of keeping them and their increase on the run until they numbered three thousand, when they would be driven off altogether? I did not boldly make such a proposal, for I had been so long occupying a false position that I was more than ever ashamed of the insignificance of my capital; but I put the case in an indirect way, just to see how he would take it. He laughed outright. 'Twelve hundred pounds indeed. Why, it would be barely sufficient to pay a year's interest on borrowed money. And the value of four hundred two-year-old ewes to be deducted into the bargain. Why, the man must be stark mad who could make such a proposition.' I never renewed the conversation, and shortly afterwards bid good-bye to the station, for I could plainly see, by my disinterested friend's altered manner, that he had guessed the true state of affairs, and wished me to take my departure. He invited me to his station in the belief that I had some thousands to invest; finding his mistake,

he desired nothing so much as to be well rid
of me.

"You are no doubt highly pleased with the
reception you have met with in Australia, and
are thoroughly convinced that squatters are the
most generous and hospitable of men. And so
they are to the chance visitor or to the Newchum
with money for investment. But tell them that,
although a gentleman by birth and education,
you are poor, and would thankfully accept any
employment on their station, they will request
you to go away.

"Not only did I bid adieu to my quondam
friend's station, but to the colony of Victoria
likewise, for I was terribly thin-skinned in those
days, and dreaded lest I should be spoken of as
the young man who wanted a share in a station
for the interest of a thousand pounds. I went
to Sydney, and after wasting six months more
in vainly hunting after respectable employment
and a safe investment for my little capital, I, in
an unlucky hour, entered into partnership
with a wide-awake individual who had succeeded
in persuading me that there was no surer way of
making money than by purchasing beasts up
country and driving them down to the Sydney
market. I wont pester you with a detailed
account of my experiences in that particular line

of business. Enough if I tell you that at the expiration of eighteen months I found myself in the streets of Sydney nearly penniless, although my partner, who had put less money than myself into the undertaking, had managed somehow or another to save sufficient to enable him to make a fresh start. I suppose that he robbed me. If so I could never discover it; but then I had implicit confidence in his honour. You see, in polite society to mistrust every man with whom one has any dealings is not considered gentlemanly. I was unfortunately a gentleman. Let a man once begin to go down hill and it seems as if all creation were greased for the occasion. Never was the truth of that saying more fully realized than in my case. Had I only known a trade—had I been taught to make horse-shoes instead of Iambics, or to handle the composing-stick instead of a double-barrel, I might perhaps have managed to weather it out. As it was, I sank lower and lower, until, to save myself from absolute starvation, I was forced to beg a shepherd's berth from F." And hiding his face in his hands, the poor fellow sobs aloud. Vainly we strive to console him. He is past consolation; and the sun begins to sink into the West, and we are forced to leave him, promising to use all our influence with his employer to

procure him a better billet.   And we mount our
horse and ride away, and turning round when a
good distance off to waive him a last adieu, we
see that he is still seated where we left him, his
head buried in his hands.   And we keep on
repeating to ourselves the poor fellow's words,
" Why did they bring me up as a gentleman?
Why was not I taught some useful trade instead
of Greek Iambics and Latin Hexameters?" &c.
And Echo answers—" Why indeed!"

The " white-handed" who leave England to
seek their fortunes at the Antipodes may be
divided into two classes.   Those who have arrived,
or are supposed to have arrived, at years of dis-
cretion, and who emigrate upon their own responsibility, and those who, fresh from school
or college, and green as grass, emigrate at the
instigation of friends or relatives.   These two
classes may be again subdivided into other two
classes—adults who emigrate because they hope
to do better in Australia than in England, and
adults who cannot possibly do any worse.
Youths who take out with them proper letters
of introduction, and whose parents are ready to
supply them with sufficient capital to commence
sheep-farming as soon as they shall have gained
the necessary experience, and youths who have
been packed off by their relatives with a hurried

"God bless you" and a cheque for a few hundreds on some Melbourne or Sydney bank. It is in the first and third categories that are to be found the lucky few; in the second and fourth the luckless many. We have already endeavoured to show how seriously a "genteel" education militates against the emigrant's chances of success, we shall now attempt to prove how absurd it is to suppose that he can turn squatter or planter with a capital of "a few hundred pounds."

We have now before us a work upon Queensland, written by a certain Mr. George Wight, a work which must have had a considerable circulation, it being the third edition. Turning to chap. viii., "How to Secure a Run," we find it stated that 750*l.* is the amount required, and that the run itself is to be secured in the following easy manner :—

"The run may be selected anywhere you like outside of those already appropriated in accordance with reasonable conditions regarding your neighbour's water frontage, &c. You ride over the portion of land you fancy, accompanied by a friend or an agent, and mark its boundaries by notching prominent trees or running your lines by creeks, or dry channels, or mountain spurs. You must see that it lies as compact as possible, for Government will not allow the pasture lands to be cut up in a wasteful manner. Starting from the furthest boundary of your neighbour's run, you thus, with the help of your friend, lay out a block of land of twenty-five square miles, and you carry in your hand a simple outline of the run, accompanied by a few sentences of a descriptive or explanatory nature to the District Commissioner. He receives you with the utmost civility, enters your application and the descriptive sentences in his large book, and even corrects your description should it be incorrect, as he knows much more about the district than you do yet. If the land is not pre-occupied—of course this is ascertained before you lodge your application—and if you are the first applicant, the Commissioner grants a licence for you to occupy the run for one year. The licence is now obtained from the District Commissioner, and within ninety days from the signing of that document you are required to pay, as an occupation fee for the year, the sum of ten shillings per square mile, and unless such fee be paid the licence is forfeited to the Crown. You may put as many sheep on your run the first year as you like, and the occupation fee, 12*l.* 10*s.*, constitutes, in fact, the rent for the year. There is one reasonable condition, and it is faithfully carried out:

during the year of licence, and at the date of application for the lease, you must have your twenty-five square mile block stocked to an extent equal to one-fourth of the number of sheep, or equivalent number of cattle, which it is deemed capable of carrying by the Act. The Government estimate is that your twenty-five square miles will carry 2500 sheep; in reality it will carry a much greater number, but the Government does not wish to be too exacting with its children, and the number, therefore, which must be depasturing on it when the application is forwarded is 625. Six hundred good sheep may be bought at the present time (1863) for less than 500*l.* The District Commissioner grants you the licence for one year. On your application the licence is converted into a fourteen years' lease on the condition mentioned by the Chief Commissioner of Crown Lands. You see what you can do with your little capital of 750*l.* were you disposed to turn squatter."

To believe Mr. Wight, there is no more difficulty in taking up new country in Australia than there would be in taking up a sheep-walk in the Highlands of Scotland. All that you have to do is to start from the furthest boundary of your neighbour's run, and, with the help of a friend, lay out a block of land of twenty-five or.

more square miles, and that done, carry a simple
outline of the run, together with a few sentences
of a descriptive or explanatory nature, to the
District Commissioner. What can possibly be
simpler? A morning's work; a week's outing at
the utmost. A man who hopes to secure a run
in the easy way described by Mr. Wight will find
himself most sorely disappointed. Should his
ride not cost him more than a couple of hundred
pounds he will have every reason to consider
himself a lucky man; if it take him no longer
time than six weeks he will be luckier still.
Before the station hunter can make the start
from "the furthest boundary of his neighbour's
run" he will have to invest largely in horse-
flesh. With less than six horses the expedition
could not well be undertaken, for the explorer
would have to be accompanied by an experienced
bushman and a couple of black boys, all of whom
would have to be mounted; and two pack-horses
would be barely sufficient to carry the rations
and the camp paraphernalia. Prices fluctuate so
in Australia that it is impossible to say how
much these six horses would be likely to cost.
When we were in the colony they could not have
been purchased for less than a couple of hundred
pounds. We will be moderate in our estimates,
and put down one hundred and twenty pounds

for horseflesh. Saddles, bridles, &c., would swallow up another thirty, so that supposing two hundred pounds to have been set aside for exploration expenses, some fifty pounds is all that would remain for wages, rations, and incidental expenses. But enough of calculations, which are necessarily unreliable. Sufficient for the would-be squatter to know that he will have to make a considerable outlay before he can start off on his explorations. We will suppose him to have arrived without mishap at the outermost station of the district in which it is his intention to squat, that his bushman is the pearl of bushmen, that his black boys are black diamonds, that his horses are all as quiet as Brighton hacks, not a bolter or buck jumper amongst them. He has made the most diligent inquiries as to the nature of the back country, whether there are any rivers or creeks, whether the feed is good and abundant, whether the blacks are troublesome, &c. &c. &c., and he is just as wise as ever. Squatters are very liberal, obliging fellows, no doubt, but to expect that they will give the first comer free gratis for nothing information which may be worth hundreds of pounds is expecting a *leetle* too much of them. It is their interest to mislead rather than to enlighten, and if the run-hunter desire to avoid being sent on a wild-goose

chase he will take the information given him
cum grano.

Anything more monotonous and wearisome
than bush exploration it would be difficult to
imagine. One day's march differs in no respect
from another day's march; describe one mile of
country, and you have described a hundred.
Unless the explorer's bump of locality be very
strongly developed he may ride a dozen times
over the same line of country without recognising
a single feature in the landscape, for it is generally the same thing over and over and over
again. Unless the party be attacked by blacks,
the chances are that from the hour of their leaving Jim-Jim or Burgoo, or whatever the name
of the outermost station may be, to the hour of
their return not a single incident will occur to
vary the dull monotony of their journey. At
daybreak each morning they will roll up their
blankets, munch a wedge of damper, gulp down
a pannikin of tea, mount their horses, and ride
hour after hour through the trackless bush.
From time to time they will halt to breathe
their horses and consult with the black boys as
to the probable whereabouts of some creek or
water-hole supposed to be on the line of march.
Satisfied on this point, they will remount their
horses and continue on their way, and what a very

weary way it is no one can form any idea who
has not ridden day after day under a tropical
sun, with nothing but tepid, turbid water to
assuage his thirst. At midday, or sooner if they
are so lucky as to stumble on a water-hole, they
will halt, hobble their horses, light a fire, cook
their dinner, bolt it, and take a siesta. At three
in the afternoon they will push on again, and
keep jogging until they reach some spot where
there is feed and water, or until it is too dark to
proceed any further. Horses hobbled or picketed,
and supper over, the black boys will coil down
for the night, whilst the white men of the party
keep watch by turns; but if the camping-ground
be in the vicinity of water, the chances are that
the sentry will not have long to keep watch alone,
he will soon be joined by his mate, from whose
eyes the mosquitoes have banished sleep. And
all through the hot, airless night they will smoke
and battle with their winged torments, and keep
longing for the morning with the same feverish
impatience as they longed for the evening during
the fervid heat of the day.

Were the run-hunter to keep a diary, a leaf
taken at random would read somewhat thus.
"January 14th, twelfth day out. Break up
camp at 5 A.M. Until 9 ride in a north-westerly
direction, hoping to strike creek spoken of by

black boys. There being no sign of any such
creek, and the country unsuited for sheep, by
Tom's advice change course to due west. 10 A.M.
Smoke seen to the northwards. Pronounced by
Charcoal to be 'black-fellows' fire,' so keep
away a point or two. No desire that they
should be apprized of our presence. 11 A.M.
Country as dry as tinder. Heat intense—fairly
reel in the saddle. Mem.: To halt at ten for
the future. 11.30. Strike creek about which so
much has been said. Dry. Follow it for a mile
or so, and find water-hole. Halt. On removing
saddles find both black boys' horses with sore
backs. Mem.: Foolish economy to buy cheap
saddles—far the dearest in the end. 3 P.M.
Boot and saddle. Follow the creek until sundown. Holes here and there along its bed, but
no depth of water. Nothing for it but to try
again. Camp."

We will suppose that he has tried again and
again, and that he has at length found that of
which he is in search—a block of well-grassed
country, having near its centre a good site for
the head station and a creek or river running
through it, with holes of sufficient depth to
insure an abundant supply of water in the driest
seasons. We will further suppose that he has
taken out his licence, and driven on to the run

not only the six hundred sheep required by the Government, but three times six hundred, and that he has still a couple of hundred pounds remaining to his credit in the bank, and then defy Mr. Wight or any other man to tell him how to tide over the first twelve months without running into debt.

Admitting that a shearing-shed can be dispensed with for the first few years, a house of some sort is indispensable, as likewise a fenced-in paddock, and unless the squatter could impress genii into his service, he would have to employ workmen. Labour is expensive in Australia. After having paid house-builders, rail-splitters, and teamsters, and provided himself with those thousand and one articles which, although they never enter into the calculations of hand-book compilers, are none the less necessary, there would be very little remaining of the two hundred pounds, and the first year's rations would have to be purchased on credit. To the ration bill must be added the wages of shepherd and hut-keeper—eighty pounds at the lowest calculation, shearer's ditto, the amount paid for carriage of wool to the nearest seaport, broker's commission, the squatter's own expenses; and to meet his liabilities he would have the wool of eighteen hundred sheep, worth, let us say, 450*l.*, a sum which would be found altogether insufficient to meet station expenses. The squatter would have no alternative but to borrow again, and to continue borrowing until such time as his clip should cover expenses.

According to the best authorities (squatting, not emigration), with less than six thousand sheep it were rash to commence sheep farming. What chance that man would have who made the attempt with six hundred, as advised by Mr. Wight, we leave the reader to imagine.

Turning from squatting to cotton-planting—chap. xvii., "Our Cotton Farm"—we find that small as is the capital required by the squatter, the cotton-planter requires even less. Provided he have a wife and two boys, aged respectively twelve and fourteen, to assist him in his labours, fifty-four pounds is sufficient, and if he go to work in the way advised by Mr. Wight, with eighteen pounds cash he will find no difficulty in raising the balance. How?—By borrowing.

Although a Scotchman, Mr. Wight has evidently no faith in the proverb—"He who goes a borrowing goes a sorrowing," for he supposes this model emigrant, whom he has taken by the hand, to have borrowed eighteen pounds from friends, and to have induced some Queensland settler to advance him other eighteen, on condition that he engage to work for him at current wages for a year—he, the employer, holding one of his land orders as security. Knowing nothing of the model emigrant's friends, we are of course unable to say whether they would be likely to lend him the money, but we have no doubt as to what the Australian squatter's response would be to such a demand. It would be in the negative. Is it probable that any employer of labour at the Antipodes would go to the trouble of assisting a man and his family to emigrate for the sake of securing their services for *one* year? And then the eighteen pound land order as security! What are these land orders?

According to Mr. Jordan, the Queensland Emigration Agent, they are "like so much money, and are available for the purchase of land on the Agricultural Reserves near all the large towns." They may be available for the purchase of land, but they most certainly are not available for the purchase of anything else. Were the emigrant to offer one of them in payment of his hotel bill the landlord would laugh in his face; and if the value of a thing can only be determined by what it will fetch in the market, land orders are worth next to nothing. On the security of one of them few men would care to advance eighteen shillings, much less pounds.

But let that pass. There are so many stumbling-
blocks in the way of Mr. Wight's model emigrant, that one more or less is of no consequence
whatsoever.

We have neither the space nor the inclination
to follow the cotton-planter step by step through
the first year's operations. We must summarize:
Mr. Wight would have the emigrant believe that
in the short pace of three months, and with the
sole assistance of two boys, he can fence his
land, build himself a small wooden hut, fell and
burn the trees on one acre of ground, and plant
it with sweet potatoes, maize, vines, pine-apples,
and bananas, and that he can besides clear and
stump two more acres for cotton. That by the
end of the first year he will have realized 18*l.*
by his cotton, have other four acres cleared and
stumped ready for planting, and maize, potatoes,
vegetables, fruit, pigs, and poultry galore for
home consumption. That the profits of his
farm the second year will be (with Government
bonus) " upwards of 300*l.*, and almost the entire
keep of the family besides, from the vegetables,
poultry, pigs, and cows which he rears."

Why not five hundred—a thousand—ten
thousand? When one has such an inexhaustible
bank as that of the imagination whereon to draw,
much better to draw for a good round sum at

once and have done with it. It takes no longer
to fill up the cheque, it looks better when it is
filled up, and the man who is simple enough to
accept the smaller sum will accept the larger.
Mr. Wight's model squatter and model cotton-
planter are of the Whittington, Robinson Suisse,
Fortunatus stamp—lucky as the first, handy as
the second, with a purse nearly as inexhaustible
as the third.

The capital of the would-be squatter is put
down at 750*l.* He pays the passage of himself
and his family to the Antipodes, and on his
arrival has still 750*l.* to the fore. He purchases
horses and gear, starts off on an exploring expedition, takes up new country, pays the board
bill of his wife and family, and is not a penny
poorer than when he landed in the colony; for
after investing 500*l.* in sheep, he has sufficient
remaining to pay his licence, meet all his installa-
tion expenses, and to purchase rations, &c., for
the first year. The experience he has gained
enables him to dispense with all assistance. He
is his own overseer and shepherd and shearer and
hurdle-maker and rail-splitter and house-builder.
He lives with his wife and children on the outermost run of the district, miles away from any
human habitation, and is as " jolly as a sand boy.'
The blacks never trouble him, the dingoes spare

his sheep, the clip of his flock pays the expenses of his station, " whilst his profits are derived from the increase (minimum 50 per cent.), with the addition of other items that advanced civilization has rendered of some value; and from being a shepherd of slender means and of little social importance, he grows up, under the blessing of Heaven, to be a squatter with enormous flocks and herds, like Abraham and Jacob, whose wealth raised envy in the breast of kings." Happy squatter!

The cotton-planter is a still more remarkable man. Wherever he goes he finds friends ready to lend him anything and everything of which he may stand in need—money, carts, harness, &c. &c. &c. Labours which would appear Herculean to most men are mere pastime to him. The rapidity with which he builds huts, runs up fencing, cuts down trees, stumps, plants, and harvests is marvellous. He thrives upon the scantiest fare, dispenses with tools and household utensils, and has his first year's crop harvested and sold before an ordinary mortal would have his seed in. By the end of the second year his farm is returning between two and three hundred pounds clear profit; and as " in succeeding years the cotton producing capabilities of the said farm may be increased to any extent by the use of white or black labour," we may say that his fortune is assured. Happy cotton-planter! Happy country! where the road to wealth is a king's highway, without rut, stone, or obstacle of any description!

But enough of fiction, let us endeavour to arrive at facts. In spite of all that may have been said and written to the contrary, the intending emigrant can rest assured that without capital his chances of success will be no greater in Australia than they would be were he to emigrate to Canada, the United States, or New Zealand—that for every instance that can be adduced of men who have commenced sheep farming or stock raising without capital, and succeeded, nine cases can be given where they have failed; and that the plums in the Australian pudding are no thicker than they are in those solid dumplings served out to the million by Brother Jonathan and Cousin Kanuc.

The first question that every man whose intention it is to emigrate to Australia should put to himself is—"Have I sufficient capital to commence sheep farming or stock raising, with a fair prospect of success?" The second—"Is the life likely to suit me?" We say sheep farming and stock raising advisedly, for not only are they in our opinion the pursuits best suited to the

gentleman emigrant of average intelligence and
limited capital, but they are almost the only ones
which can be followed without loss of caste.

The squattocracy constitute the aristocracy of
Australia, and for no man has the squatter a
more supreme contempt than for the agriculturist·
That the soil of all five provinces is adapted to
the growth of cereals—and that in Queensland
cotton, sugar, and tobacco can be raised to perfection, we do not for one moment deny ; but what
the emigrant has to consider is not whether this
or that product can be grown in Australia, but
whether it can be grown to *greater* profit than
elsewhere.   On the calculations of the ordinary
hand-book compiler no reliance can be placed,
for they are based on suppositions and not on
facts.   It is always *presuming* that one man and
a boy can cultivate ten acres of Sea Island
cotton, and *presuming* that it is worth one shilling
and threepence per pound, and *presuming* that
there will be a constant demand for that particular staple, the net profit per acre *should be*, &c.

We cannot presume anything of the kind.
With all due deference to the opinions of the
Director of the Brisbane Botanic Garden, Dr.
Hobbs, and other eminent Colonial authorities,
we beg to offer counter evidence in the shape of
the "American Farm Book," written by R. L.

Allen, Editor of the *American Agriculturist.*
What does Mr. Allen say on the subject of Sea
Island cotton?

"The cultivation of Sea Island cotton is carried
on by the hand hoe, and *the quantity is always
limited to four acres to the labourer.* Five hundred
pounds per acre is the medium crop, which at
twenty cents per pound is to the planter $100
for gross crop; and from this $100 is to be
subtracted bagging, freight, expenses of sale,
clothing for his people, medical attendance, and;
too often, provisions. When the seed was first
introduced, it was planted in hills prepared upon
the level field at five feet each way; but it was
soon found to be a very tender plant, liable to
suffer by storms of wind, by drought, by excess
of rain. Many changes have come over this seed
since that time, from difference of soil, culture,
and local position, and above all, from careful
selection of seed. But the cause is yet to be
discovered why the gain in fineness of wool is lost
in the quality and weight of the product; for in
spite of a zeal and intelligence brought to act
upon the subject without parallel, the crops are
yearly diminishing, until *to grow Sea Island cotton
is one of the most profitless pursuits within the limits
of the United States.*"

In a work published by us some seven years

since, we expressed our doubts as to Dr. Lang's industrious and virtuous Queensland cotton-planter being able to enter into successful competition with the American free negro, and time has proved that we were not far wrong. Dr. Lang's prophecies, like those of Dr. Cumming, do not seem to "come off," and his dream of Queensland being the future cotton field of England, is as far from realization as ever. England's cotton field is wherever the fibre can be grown at the least cost, and that is not in Queensland; and to suppose that Manchester manufacturers would consent to give a halfpenny a pound more for their cotton in order to encourage Colonial enterprise, is as absurd as to imagine that the abolitionist would pay fourpence halfpenny a pound for "free"-grown sugar, when slave-grown can be purchased for fourpence farthing.

Whether the climate of Queensland is better adapted to the growth of cotton than the Southern States—whether one Queenslander can cultivate as much land as two negroes—whether the demand for Sea Island cotton will increase or diminish the price, rise or fall, we shall not stop to consider. That the cotton raised in the colony in 1871 amounted to only 1,487,000lbs. is quite sufficient for us.

The cotton fever is over, the cane fever has set

in ; sugar, it appears, not cotton, is to be the future staple of Queensland ; and those who have sufficient money to pay their passage to the colony, are earnestly invited by the Colonial Government to take up land, plant canes and make their fortunes, just as they were invited to become] cotton-planters, and do the same ten years ago. The profits to be derived from cane growing are prodigious. The sugar that sells for 34l. per ton can be made for 12l. 10s. The canes from an acre of land yield from fourteen cwt. to three tons of sugar—and there are molasses and rum into the bargain. Little capital is required— clearing, fencing, and stumping costs from 7l. to 20l. per acre ; and you need not manufacture the sugar yourself, but have it made for you by con- tract at from 10l. to 12l. per ton.

Now, it seems to us that there is more than one obstacle in the road of the cane-planter who has his sugar made by contract. Unlike wheat, maize, and other products which can be stacked until such time as the farmer can thrash and garner—cane must be hauled to the mill as soon as cut, be ground and converted into sugar; for un- less the weather be cold, which it rarely is in ·Queensland, acetic fermentation soon takes place, and the syrup will not crystallize.

Unless the mill came to the planter, the

planter would have to haul his cane to the mill.
How far would he have to haul it? and what
would it be likely to cost him per ton? How
would he manage so that his sugar-making might
not interfere with the sugar-making of the man
who contracted for the job? He could not well
retard the ripening of his cane, when ripe it
would have to be cut, when cut, ground and
made into sugar—would he wait? or would the
contractor? Supposing that the individual who
owned the mill and the sugar-house had no plantation of his own, that he was district miller and
sugar-boiler, how would he manage to give satisfaction to all his customers? for to make his establishment a paying concern he would require a good
number. He could not work for all at the same
time, some of them would have to wait; would
they draw lots or fight for turns? or how?—would
the man whose sugar turned out a *fiasco* be com-
pensated by those whose sugar was A1?

We are no doubt very obtuse, but try in which
way we will we cannot work it out. The needy
cane grower who had neither mill nor sugar-
house, would, it seems to us, be much more likely
to work for the benefit of his mill-owning neighbour than for his own. Who guarantees him
that he can always have his sugar made by con-.
tract? Supposing that no one would undertake

the job—what then ?   He would have to sell his crop for whatever sum the said mill-owning neighbour might be pleased to offer him, or let it rot on the ground where it stood.   What would he be likely to get per acre for his crop? and would that sum be sufficient to cover all expenses and leave a profit?   That is what the ordinary settler would desire to know, not whether steam ploughs are preferable to horse ploughs, or vacuum pans to Hart's patent.   The inducements held out to the emigrant read very well.   That the "government of Queensland offers the pick of 1000 miles of coast line, by about twenty in breadth, with numerous creeks, rivers, bays, and inlets, for selection by sugar-planters, at prices varying from five to fifteen shillings per acre, with a credit extending over ten years," sounds excessively liberal.   But before the land is in a condition to receive the cane, it must be cleared and stumped and fenced and ploughed, at a cost of, say 15*l.* per acre.   Fifteen pounds for clearing, fifteen shillings for the land.

Does it not strike the reader, that the man who could find the pounds would in all probability be able to find the odd shillings? and that if there was anything in it the terms offered are too liberal by half?   Our own experience is that extraordinary bargains are, in ninety-nine cases

out of a hundred, extraordinary catchpennies—
that whatever is worth having is worth paying for; and we confess that we have as little
faith in the success of the Queensland cane-
planter (impecunious) as we had in Dr. Lang's
model cotton-planter ten years ago.

With the capitalist it is different. Provided
he has sufficient capital to commence operations
on a tolerably extensive scale—to purchase the
best machinery and the most approved labour-
saving implements; and provided he has served
his time to the business, or can secure a first-class
man as overseer; and provided he can obtain
field-hands on the spot—that he be not obliged
to charter a schooner to kidnap South Sea Is-
landers whenever the supply falls short—there is
no reason why he should not do as well as the
Louisianian planter. Sugar commands a high
price in the colony—there is a market on the
spot—land is cheap—*presuming the data to be reliable* the Queensland sugar-planter ought to be
pretty certain of making handsome profits. But
are the data reliable? Can land, at the present
high rate of labour, be cleared and stumped and
fenced and cultivated at an average cost of
13*l.* 10*s.* an acre? Can sugar be manufactured at
12*l.* 10*s.* a ton? and is the *average* yield one ton
and a-half per acre? We do not wish to be cap-

tious, but, like the Dutchman afore-mentioned,
we cannot help thinking that the reports are
"moch doo gut do be drue."

Turning from planting to farming, what are
the advantages which the Australian farmer
possesses over his American brother? We can
well imagine how perplexed the intending emigrant must be after reading a dozen contradictory statements on the subject. Mr. Wight in-
forms him that in Queensland two and even
three crops of maize, worth from 4*s*. 6*d*. to 5*s*. a
bushel, can be grown in the year, and forty
bushels of wheat to the acre, the said wheat
"yielding a profit (taking the average of seasons) of about 8*s*. per bushel, when made into
flour, supposing flour to be worth in Warwick
3*l.* per bag of 200lbs. The maize must be of a
different variety to that grown in America, or
indeed anywhere else; for he proceeds to inform
his readers that the "Indian corn-flour of Queensland is much more palatable than the Indian
corn-flour which the poor Irish had doled out to
them a few years ago as a substitute for the
potato;" and "that no one would have believed
a short time ago that *maize and wheat could grow
within the same range of climate.*" It is a pity
that there should be such a limited demand for
the former product, it being evidently a more

profitable crop than either cotton or sugar, although not quite perhaps so profitable as the banana, which is said to realize an average return of not less than 40l. per acre.

Having no price-current list to refer to we are unable to say what flour may now be fetching per sack in Brisbane, but unless the bakers sell at a loss, it cannot be worth 3l. or even 2l. a sack in Victoria; for according to another authority (emigration), bread in Melbourne ranges from a penny halfpenny to a penny three-farthings per pound—cheaper than in London—with flour at thirty-two shillings the barrel.

But even admitting that the Australian farmer gets one-third more for his wheat than does the Canadian, his profits are smaller; for, whilst paying twenty per cent. more for his labour, the yield of his land is considerably less. The fact of this or that man having thrashed out forty bushel to the acre proves nothing. It is not what one man or fifty men may have done, but what colonial farmers as a body do on the average. We happen to know the gentleman to whom Mr. Wight refers—Mr. Fleming, of Ipswich. He has, or had when we were in Queensland, a "boiling-down" establishment, and could, had he been so minded, have top-dressed his

sixty acres to the depth of a foot with garbage,
and it is this man, of all others, whose land
we are requested to take as a criterion. We re-
spectfully decline to do anything of the sort, or
to accept as an authority on colonial farming a
man who is so ignorant of the products of the
habitable globe as to express surprise that maize
and wheat can grow within the same range of
climate.

We prefer taking the opinion of a Canadian
friend of ours, a practical farmer, who has recently returned from Australia, more especially
as his experiences coincide with our own and
with those of every *disinterested* Colonial whom
we have questioned on the subject. After travelling through the three colonies of Victoria, New
South Wales, and Queensland—using his eyes
and ears the while—he is of opinion that, taking
one year with another, the yield of wheat is not
the third of forty bushels per acre, whilst the cost
of production is fully twenty per cent. more than
in Canada West.

The climate being one of extremes—not of
heat and cold as in Canada, but of rain and
drought, which is infinitely worse—the yield is
more unequal than in other countries—one year
it is abundant, another it hardly pays the cost of
production. To a certain extent the same can

be said of the harvest in all countries; but the Australian farmer is differently situated to most other farmers, in that, in losing his wheat crop, he loses well nigh all. Should his wheat be thin, the Canadian farmer can generally console himself with the reflection that his root or hay crop is first-rate, or that his oats and barley are above the average; for the weather that is injurious to the one is apt to be good for the others, and *vice versâ*. What he loses here he gains there. Not so the Australian husbandman—wheat is his sheet-anchor, and when it goes the ship goes too, unless there be another anchor in the shape of a reserve fund, which there very often is not. For this reason Australia can hardly be called "a good poor man's country." Unless his passage out be in part paid—unless he gets his land gratis, and is allowed to fence and clear it at his own convenience ; unless he be, in fact, a Government immigrant, such as we have attempted to describe in our opening chapter, he is, in our opinion, much more likely to succeed in the United States or Canada, for the same amount which would be required to pay his passage, and start him in a small way in Australia, would be amply sufficient to give him a good start in either country, whilst the risk run is infinitely less. Australia is a fairly good country for the practical working farmer who has a capital of at least five hundred pounds; it is a very good one for the gentleman emigrant (unmarried), who has at least five thousand. It is not a country where the impecunious emigrant can take up twenty or forty acres of land and live on the produce thereof; nor one where the gentleman emigrant can live at his ease on the interest of a few thousand pounds.

Australia is a fine country — a very fine country, but it is not precisely the sort of country to which any sane man would emigrate in order to enjoy his *otium cum dig.*; and if to make money be not his object, he has no business there. We never yet met the squatter whose affection for the land of his adoption was such that he desired to be buried there. One and all had the same end in view—to make their pile, and the sooner the better, and return to Europe. There may be hundreds and thousands of men who prefer Australia to England—the bush to either London or Paris; but we can truthfully say that we never encountered one of them on our travels; and for our own part we should have considered the man who professed to do so a fit inmate for a lunatic asylum. "Needs must when the devil drives;" but when he no longer drives, when an independence has been secured, that man must be more than eccentric who would remain in a country which possesses so few attractions for the man of leisure. We do not say this to disparage the country, but in order that the emigrant may distinctly understand that Australia is not altogether the Arcadia it has been represented. We have no object in running down the colony. Neither are we a victimized Newchum, nor a disappointed gold-seeker, nor a bankrupt sheep farmer. We never invested one penny in stock or flock, nor have we any intention of making the venture. No Australian, so far as we can remember, ever did us an injury; on the contrary, many were the kindnesses we received at the hands of squatters and others during our stay in the country. If we could conscientiously do so we should only be too happy to endorse the statements of Dr. Lang and other colonial writers, and say to the intending emigrant, "Australia is a terrestrial paradise; go, and your welfare is assured." A province of the British empire, we should much prefer seeing our fellow-countrymen flocking thither than to the dominions of Uncle Samuel. But unfortunately it is not what may be gratifying to us as a Briton that has to be considered, but what may be beneficial to them as emigrants, and we should not be doing our duty did we not warn our

readers against placing confidence in the highly
coloured descriptions of colonial pamphleteers,
and tell them plainly that Australia, although
under certain conditions a very good country, is,
as a place of residence, far—very far behind
Canada and the United States. As we cannot
give our reasons for making this assertion without going twice over the same ground, we shall,
as we proceed, attempt to describe Australian
bush life in the same way that we have described
life in the Canadas and the United States, leaving
it to the reader to compare the two, and discover
these reasons by inference.

The financial question being satisfactorily
settled, the next point for consideration is the
emigrant's fitness for the life he has in view.
Hunting and shooting, and rowing and fishing,
are doubtless very manly accomplishments,
being able to rough it a great desideratum in a
country where there are few inns at which to
take one's ease, and where the settlers' houses
are miles apart; but it is a great mistake to
imagine that an aptitude for field sports, and
toughness, is all that is necessary to make the
squatter. That breeding will tell—that the
gentleman will often uncomplainingly endure
hardships that would make Hodge throw up the
sponge—we admit, but these hardships must be

of reasonable duration; when it come to cart-horse work, the yokel has generally the best of it. Were the field of fortune a racecourse, and the prizes awarded to the fleetest over a short stretch, the thoroughbreds would have it all their own way. But the prize is not to the swiftest, but to the most enduring, and the most enduring are not always the thoroughbred; and the question that the gentleman emigrant has to put to himself is not, "Have I the pace?" but "Have I the endurance—the endurance to lead the lonely existence of a squatter for fifteen or twenty long years?"

Supposing the answer to be in the affirmative, our friend's first move should be to obtain letters of introduction to some of the colonial squatting notabilities; for although such letters are for the most part purely formal, they may be of service, and they cannot well do any harm. Unless the emigrant be a very young man, there is no occasion for his being consigned, or for his consigning himself, to any particular squatter or leader and general manager desirous of "taking out pupils." We don't believe in the premium arrangement—giving one or two hundred pounds to be permitted to "gain experience" on this or that man's run; still less in the throw-in-your-lot-amongst-us-let-us-all-have-one-purse programme. The man who pays a premium for being taught station routine, pays money for being permitted to do work for which he ought properly to be paid; and the man who throws in his lot with a party of young fellows of whose characters and dispositions he knows nothing, is very likely to grow heartily weary of the partnership before six months have rolled over his head.

Getting a number of young men to subscribe a certain amount of capital for the purchase of a sheep station, the said sheep station to be worked for their mutual benefit by an irresponsible leader and general manager, who receives a salary of seven or eight hundred per annum for his services, is a capital arrangement for the "irresponsible manager," but we don't exactly see how the shareholders are likely to benefit by it. The very fact of a fixed salary being demanded ought to put men on their guard; for if Mr. Manager had any faith in his own management he would much prefer that his remuneration should be made dependent on the gross profits of the run. There are plenty of first-rate managers who would be only too happy to enter into such an arrangement; and if an overseer were sufficient, his wages ought not to exceed a hundred and twenty or a hundred and fifty pounds per annum. That three or four friends

might find it to their interest to club their money
for the purchase of a station we can readily
believe, but that a dozen men, total strangers to
each other, would find it answer to do the same
we cannot. There would be a squabble and a
dissolution of partnership before the end of the
first year; for to suppose that grown-up men
would consent to submit their differences to
their paid manager is almost as absurd as to
suppose that they would entrust him with a
capital of thirty or forty thousand pounds without first obtaining substantial security.

Instead of paying a premium to be allowed to
do loblolliboy's work on a station, or making an
arrangement with some wide-awake ex-manager
to be taken out as a "pupil," the adult emigrant
should, on his arrival in the colony, lodge his
capital in the Bank of Australasia or New South
Wales (a much safer place than any man's
pocket), and spend a month or two in looking
about him. Unless things have very much
altered since we were in the country, he will not
have to look very far to find a squatter ready to
take him without premium; for let Mr. Newchum be never so green, his services are worth
more than his rations. It may be to his advantage to accept such an offer, and it may not; all
will depend on the state of his banker's account,

and for this reason—the only men likely to make such a proposal will be pioneer or up-country squatters, doing business on a limited scale, and to whom every pound is a matter of consequence. Their object in taking him will be, not that he may have the opportunity of gaining experience for his own future benefit, but that he may make himself useful on the station, and save the wages of one paid hand. They will tell him, no doubt, that his duties will be limited to riding about the station, weighing the rations, and such light commissions. But once there, he will be expected to work like a nigger, and turn his hand to anything and everything, from sheep-washing to cooking the men's dinners. The experience he will gain on such a station will be of the rough and ready kind—the experience necessary for the pioneer squatter; and if to take up new country be his intention, he could not go to a better place.

If, on the other hand, he have capital to pur-chase an improved run, where everything goes by clockwork, and where method and order take the place of shifts and expedients, he could not well go to a worse. It is only on first-class stations, or those represented to be such, that a premium is demanded; the up-country squatter is generally perfectly willing to accept Mr.

Newchum's services as payment in full for his rations, and even then he has by far the best of the bargain. This being the case, it will be naturally imagined that the man who pays a premium enjoys greater privileges and immunities than he who pays none. But it is not so. As a rule there is little or no difference in the treatment. The " Colonial experience" young man must come when he is called and go when he is sent, and perform any task that it may be the good pleasure of his master, the squatter, or of his vice, the manager, to set him. If he doesn't like it he can go about his business, and of course sacrifice the money he has paid as premium. The squatter would say, no doubt, that it is only by turning his hand to everything that he can gain experience, and this to a certain extent is true enough. But there is a limit to all things. That Mr. Newchum should be in turn shepherd, cow-tailer, sheep-washer, fleece-rolier, butcher, dry-salter, ration carrier, and cook is very proper. But to understand how sheep are folded it is not necessary that he should be packed off to an out-station for months on a stretch to keep hut for a German shepherd; the art of sheep-washing can be acquired without standing the livelong day up to one's waist in the soak-hole; to learn how rations are carried it is not indispensable to become carrier to the station, nor how damper is made, cook. And yet it is at these and similar occupations that the young fellow is generally kept pottering during the entire term of his apprenticeship. When he should be riding round the station with the overseer he is ration-carrying; shepherding when he ought to be keeping the station accounts. His are the jobs and errands that no one else cares to take, his the shoulders upon which the blame rests when anything goes wrong on the station. Has a horse a sore back? "It was Mr. Newchum as giv' it him." Does a sheep get drowned at the soak-hole? "Mr. N. C.'s d—d carelessness again." Is anything lost, strayed, or stolen? "Mr. N. C.'s fault, you may be sure." Every one on the station, from the squatter or manager downwards, thinks Mr. Newchum fair game. Were Mr. Squatter to speak to his German or Scotch shepherd or to his colonial-raised bullock-driver in the same tone as he addresses Mr. Newchum, he would be politely requested to go to Halifax and to find another servant. Poor Newchum, whilst inwardly burning with indignation, ventures not a word in reply, for he knows how difficult it will be, in the event or dismissal, to find another billet.

We do not deny that the squatter's temper is

occasionally severely tried by acts of omission and commission on the part of the Colonial experience young man—it is only what might be expected. You "can't make a silk purse out of a sow's ear," nor an experienced bushman out of the recently landed greenhorn. It takes time to learn a trade, and to call a man a stupid muff because he is not an expert at a business to which he has served no apprenticeship is absurd. "Every man to his place, and the cook to the fore-sheet." Jack passing the weather earring in a gale of wind is a fine smart fellow; put him astride of a buckjumper instead of a yard-arm and what is he? and were the Colonial experience young gentleman to be the admirable Crichton himself, he would be a stupid muff in the eyes of the one-idead squatter. To assert, as many squatters and managers do assert, that nine-tenths of the young fellows who leave England to better themselves in the colonies are either idiots, shirks, or prodigals is a gross libel, and were any ex-squatter or manager to make such a statement in our hearing we would give him the lie direct. At the very least calculation three-fifths of the body are ready and willing to work, and would prove recognisant for any little kindness shown them. But considerate treatment is what they very seldom get. If they pay a premium, the amount will barely cover the damage done to flock and stock by their carelessness and stupidity. If they pay no premium, but give their services as a set-off against their rations, it is out of sheer compassion that they are permitted to remain on the station.

If they take wages, they belong to the white-handed class—they are above their business; they are not worth their salt; an Irish Mickey is worth a dozen of them, and so forth. It is not by treating men after this fashion that the squatter can hope to secure their faithful services. No squatter is by law compelled to take one of the white-handed; but when he chooses to do so, he ought to treat him, if not precisely as an equal, at least as a being who has a soul in his body, which, in nine cases out of ten, he does not. The consequence too often is that the man becomes indifferent, careless, sulky, and dismisses himself, or is dismissed, from the station. If he have some capital upon which to fall back, he forfeits the money he has paid as premium, and there is an end of the matter; but if he have little or no money, if he be dependent on his family for the means of subsistence, the step is generally a fatal one. His first move will be to write a letter to the governor or to his elder brother, uncle, guardian, or whoever may stand *in loco parentis*, giving a detailed account of the causes which have led to his leaving his situation, winding up with an appeal for a little pecuniary assistance. His next to endeavour to find employment. In the hopes of being able to obtain a clerkship, he most probably goes to Melbourne, or Sydney, or Brisbane; but, on making inquiries, he finds that no one is in want of a clerk. He is not proud; he will undertake the duties of shopman, timekeeper, messenger. Ten applicants for every place vacant. He will act as rough-rider, cab-driver, drayman. No one in need of his services. There are only two employments open to him—road work and station work; and as he knows nothing of the noble art of stone-breaking, he engages as shepherd or hut-keeper to some up-country squatter. It will not be for long, he thinks to himself as he humps his pack and starts on his weary tramp. In four months at the furthest he will receive an answer to his letters, accompanied by a remittance, and then good-bye to Australia. But when the anxiously expected letter does at length make its appearance, the poor fellow finds, to his bitter disappointment, that instead of a remittance, it contains a homily. The writer is surprised and shocked that he—Tom, Dick, or Harry—should have the presumption to ask for further assistance. Did he not, on leaving England, receive two hundred—five hundred—a thousand pounds? —(this, in the case of the young gentleman having been " shepherded," or induced to invest his little capital in some ruinous undertaking)—amply sufficient, according to competent authorities, to commence sheep-farming, cotton-planting, cane-growing. Why has he not put his shoulder to the wheel instead of spending his money in dissipation? No use writing long stories about capital being insufficient, runs of ill-luck, or that he has been swindled out of his money. No one believes his statements. *According to the very best authorities* the capital provided was more than ample; swindlers are the creation of his fertile imagination; bad luck is invariably the result of bad conduct. As he has made his bed so he must lie on it. He must not expect any further assistance from his family. He, the writer, has a certain position to keep up (younger sons and brothers are never supposed to have any social position or status), and the estate is barely sufficient to enable him to do so respectably. All that he can do for him is to pray, &c. &c. &c. Or—Did not he, the peti-tioner, receive one hundred pounds and a com-plete outfit, and was not another hundred paid to Mr. Sheepshanks that he might gain experience on his station? That he has left owing to bad treatment is all nonsense; Mr. S. being, by all accounts, a most estimable, kind-hearted man, and utterly incapable of acting in the manner that has been represented. If any unpleasant-ness has arisen, it must have been entirely owing to the petitioner's own bad conduct. To send him money would only be to encourage him in his evil courses. It is only by eating the bread of adversity that he can be brought to see the error of his ways, &c. &c. &c.

During our Australian wanderings scarcely a week passed without our encountering some unhappy victim to parental infatuation—to call it by no harsher name—who, with tears in his eyes, would confide to us the story of his misfor-tunes, and not unfrequently beg us to read the letters which he had received from home in answer to his applications for assistance. In no one single instance, so far as we can remember, did the parent take any portion of the blame on his own shoulders; and it was very rarely that he even admitted that his son had been unfortunate and not vicious. It was almost invariably the youth's own fault, and the father majestically washed his hands of all responsibility. Now, if the parent was occasionally right in his conjec-tures, it is not too much to say that, in the

majority of cases, he was wrong—that pro-
fligacy and obstinacy had nothing to do with his
son's misfortunes—that the young fellow had
done his best and failed, as men will fail who
have no experience.

Does it never strike parents that the same
qualities which are requisite to insure success at
home, are doubly so abroad? and that the
youth who, owing to the imperfect development
of his bumps of acquisitiveness, cautiousness,
firmness, and order, is unlikely to make much
headway in England, is morally certain to drift
to leeward in Australia? How often will they
require to be told that no greater folly—no
greater cruelty can be committed, than that of
packing off their shiftless, penniless, younger
sons to the Antipodes to make their fortunes
by squatting, cotting-planting, farming, and
what not? That only two classes of emigrants
are at present required in Australia—those who
have been brought up to hard work and those
who have capital for investment, and that no
credence is to be placed in the so-called "hand-
books" to the colonies, they being compiled either
by paid emigration agents or by men who desire to curry popularity by "writing-up" the
land of their adoption? If it has been told them
once, it has been told them a score of times, and

yet, in spite of all that has been said and written on the subject, they will persist in sending out their sons to what they must well know is almost certain perdition. What their reason may be in giving such a decided preference to Australia we know not, but this much we know—that any father who packs off his son to the Antipodes without first providing him with sufficient money to make a fair start, is as guilty of that son's death, if any evil befall him, as though he had knocked him on the head with a handspike.

Of all countries in the world Australia is the one where the descent to Avernus is the easiest. Between dapper Richard Newchum, Esquire, passenger per *Great Britain*, and Dick the dirty, ragged, unkempt shepherd, on Boggin's station, there is but one step; for without a trade and without money the shepherding is merely a question of time. In the United States there is a constant demand for help—help which is not menial—and the young man who is smart, sober, and willing has not to search very far to find a job of some description. In Australia the demand is limited to skilled artisans, domestic servants, farm labourers, and station hands; for every other vacant situation there is a hundred applicants. Station or road work is Mr. Newchum's alternative—a nice alternative for a gentleman truly.

"Why doesn't Dick find some respectable employment?" sighs paterfamilias, as he sniffs his glass of old Tawny and warms his gouty toes at the blazing seacoal fire.

"Too difficult to please, perhaps," suggests Mr. Elder Brother, helping himself to an olive.

Respectable employment! Difficult to please!! Independent!!! Could paterfamilias only behold poor Dick mournfully munching his damper outside the wretched hovel that shelters him from the weather, his port might, perchance, have a little less bouquet; and could Mr. Primogeniture be only compelled to take Brother Dick's billet for a twelvemonth, what a vast amount of good! But we are drifting into the younger son question, and as it is one we desire to avoid we will return to the gentleman immigrant proper, or capitalist, and leave the gentleman improper, or capital-less, to his damper and his despair.

Before accepting the offer of rations in exchange for services, the "Colonial Experiencer" should come to a thorough understanding with Mr. Squatter as to what those services are to be. If "making himself useful" mean taking the place of a paid hand, doing duty as shepherd,

ration-carrier, hut-keeper, &c., he should refuse
point blank. If, on the contrary, it mean attend-
ing store, keeping the station accounts, counting
sheep, and working on and around the head
station, it would be to his decided advantage to
accept. In the event of his being unable to find
a squatter willing to take him on these terms,
he might offer to pay for being allowed to reside
on the station, not one or two hundred pounds
cash down as premium, but so much a year, the
money to be paid quarterly or half-yearly in
advance. By making some such arrangement as
this, not only will he retain his independence,
but the squatter, having nothing to gain by his
departure, will be much more likely to treat him
with consideration.

We will suppose that he has gained his experience, and that he is about to commence
sheep farming on his own account. The first
thing he wants is a run. No difficulty in obtaining one now-a-days.* Hundreds of runs in the
market, all to be sold for one-half their real value.
When we were in Australia not a squatter was
there in the country who would have dreamt of
taking less than one pound per head for his sheep
(station thrown in); twenty-five shillings was a
common price. Now, it would appear, that he

---

* 1871.

who can get eight or ten shillings considers himself lucky. Any man who had in those days ventured to prophesy the present state of things would have been hooted. The Australian world had gone squatting mad. Sheep runs were the real Australian gold fields; the fortune of the man who possessed one was assured. Every man who had a few hundred pounds went in for sheep farming. Immense tracts of new country were taken up and stocked with sheep that would have been dear at a gift; money was borrowed at usurious interest to carry on the work. The clips being of inferior quality, did not fetch sufficient to cover expenses. The squatters were unable to meet their liabilities; the mortgagees foreclosed, and station after station was thrown on the market. The supply exceeding the demand, station property went down, down, down, until the market value of sheep was very little above "pot" price, or the amount they would realize if boiled down and converted into tallow.

It was then that men discovered to their cost that 750l. was not sufficient to commence sheep farming, that borrowing money did not pay, that first-class returns could only be obtained by first-class management, and that the larger the station the greater the proportionate profits. The " strong" squatters, those who had the where-

withal to purchase the best imported stock,
whose clip, instead of being sold for eightpence
or tenpence a pound, fetched eighteenpence or
two shillings, whose stations were conducted
on the most approved principles, these men
held their own, whilst those who had small runs
stocked with coarse-woolled sheep, and who were
working with borrowed money, were tumbled
over like ninepins.

Whether sheep will ever be lower than they
are at present it is impossible to say, but it is
not probable. At present prices station property
ought to be a safe investment, provided the
purchase-money has not to be borrowed, and
provided there be judicious management. To
secure a first-rate run it might be to a man's
advantage to give bills for a portion of the
purchase-money, but unless under exceptional
circumstances these bills ought never to exceed
one-third of the entire amount. Australian
estate agents are, as regards the accepting of
bills, the most obliging fellows in existence. If
you have a couple of thousand in cash, and are
willing to give bills at three or more years' date
for the other six, you can walk into the possession
of a station worth six or eight thousand pounds.
If you can't meet the bills as they fall due, all
that you will have to do is to walk off again.

Easiest thing in the world. The chances against you are not greater than they would be at *trente et quarante*. You may win, but the *refait* in the shape of interest is very likely to upset your little martingale, whatever it may be.

Our immigrant, being by this time wide awake, it is to be hoped pays cash down for his station, receiving the abatement usual in such cases. Where his station may be, whether in Victoria, New South Wales, or Queensland, matters not a straw; what the precise number of sheep on his run is of no consequence to the reader. Over six thousand, under twenty, he can fix the number to suit himself. Mounted on a stout roadster, with valise strapped in front of him, behold him starting from Melbourne, Sydney, Brisbane, on his up-country ride, a little journey of two hundred miles or more.

Four hours' riding brings him to Soakem's Inn, twenty odd miles from the city, and here he dismounts to bait his horse and get some dinner. Soakem's differs in no respect from the generality of Australian road-side inns—it is a pot-house with the pretensions of a hotel. There is a small dining-room, where breakfasts, dinners, and suppers are served up to the hungry traveller by Mrs. S.; and a large bar, where liquor is dispensed by Mr. S. to the thirsty one. As a

hundred to one, so are the thirsty to the hungry;
for each meal prepared by the hostess a hundred
glasses of liquor are served over the counter by
her lord. The dining-room is often vacant; the
tap never. From rosy morn until dewy eve, and
from dewy eve until black midnight, there is a
constant demand for "nobblers," nobblers of
rum and nobblers of gin, nobblers of whisky and
nobblers of brandy, for Australian bullock-drivers
and stockmen hold milder liquor in contempt.
Alcohol is what they affect, and the more fiery
it is the better. Right good customers are these
same bullock-drivers and stockmen to Mr. Soakem, but they are not his best. Our host's most
profitable customers are shepherds, hut-keepers,
and station hands, who take their money in a
lump, and horse-breakers, rail-splitters, shearers,
&c., who are paid by the job. When Soakem
espies one of these worthies crossing his hospitable threshold his heart rejoices greatly, for he
knows that the new-comer is in possession of a
cheque, which cheque ought, by the laws of bush
gravitation, to pass from the greasy pocket-book
where it reposes to a certain fire-proof safe behind
the counter, and he is rarely disappointed. On
the third, fourth, fifth day, according to the size
of his cheque (it is a stiff one that will last a
week), Mr. Shepherd wakes up from a drunken

sleep, and asks, as usual, for an "eye-opener" in the shape of a nobbler. It is refused him.

Why can't he have it?

Because he has already received the full value of his cheque, and mine host does not care to give credit to strangers.

The value of his cheque! Why, it was for four-and-twenty pounds!! Can't have drunk twenty-four pounds' worth of liquor in five days?

If he hasn't his pals have. Old French brandy can't be dipped out of the creek; and when a cove goes in for that there kind of tipple he must pay for it. Does he think that he, John Soakem, would cheat him? Better keep a civil tongue in his head, or he will be put out of the house.

Put out of the house he generally is, and morning finds him once again on the station from which he so lately set forth, a sadder, but seldom a wiser man.

After a couple of hours' rest our squatter con- tinues on his way, and a very uninteresting way it is. No snow-capped peak or purple mountain; no rushing river or purling stream; no limpid lake or crystal fountain; no shady forest or mossy bank, not so much as a hedgerow to relieve the eye, or a village spire to enliven the prospect—nothing but a long stretch of road, dusty or muddy, as the case may be, with gum-trees on one side and gum-trees on the other, with here and there a fenced in lot and slab-hut of some enterprising settler. Like an English park, indeed! The country has as much resemblance to an English park as it has to the garden of Eden.

It being a main road, there is a considerable amount of traffic along it. Wool-laden drays drawn by eight yoke of panting oxen, going down ; ditto, laden with stores, going up. Drovers with fat beasts for the pots or markets, city or station-bound squatters on horseback, and the usual complement of pack-laden pedestrians—shepherds, hut-keepers, rail-splitters, &c., in search of employment.

Towards sundown our squatter reaches Y——, the station where he is to pass the night. Y—— is one of the largest and best managed stations in the province, and everything on and around it bears evidence to a liberal outlay of capital. The run has been to a great extent fenced in, wells have been sunk to supply the flocks and herds with water, and wool-sheds and drafting-yards of the most approved description erected. In the home-paddocks, imported stock, to the value of some thousands of pounds, is grazing. Bulls of distinguished pedigree ; rams which ought, from the price paid for them, to yield a golden fleece ;

stallions, own brothers to this or to that Two
Thousand Guineas or Leger winner.

It is a treat to walk round the head station
with the manager and listen to him expatiating
on the merits of his favourites, to see the order
and regularity prevailing in every department,
and equally so to return to the house, the tour of
inspection over, and sit down to that rarest of all
rare things in the bush, a well-cooked, well-served
dinner.

Very different is the head station at Y—— to
the generality of Australian head stations. The
house has been built with a due regard to comfort; the rooms are lofty and well furnished,
there is a library for the studiously disposed, a
piano for the musical, and a garden tastefully
laid out with shrubs and flowers wherein to
smoke one's calumet of peace after the labours
of the day are over. When our squatter thinks
how very rough and ready is the accommodation
of his own up-country station he cannot suppress
a feeling of envy. Could he only enter into
possession of just such another station as Y——
how happy and contented he would be. So at
least he fancies. But were he the owner of a
station worth a hundred thousand pounds, it is
more than probable that he likewise would
engage a manager and live in Europe; for what,

after all, is the use of having money if the privilege of spending it be denied one.

Our friend's second day's ride is just as uninteresting as his first. Were it not that the road is very much worse, the fences fewer, and the public-houses further apart, it might be yesterday's ride over again. Gum-trees, gum-trees, gum-trees. A cloud of dust, and half-a-dozen wool-laden drays groaning, creaking, swaying in the deep ruts, the drivers cursing and swearing as only Australian bullock-drivers can. A flock of sheep, the gentle shepherd, with cutty instead of Pandean pipe, his crook a bludgeon. A mob of kangaroo bounding away across the open. An iguana basking in the sun. A flock of screaming cockatoo. A scrub. A gully with the bones of many a stout bullock lying scattered around. A party of dusty, sunburnt station-hands on the tramp. Iron-bark trees. An encampment of bullock drays. A public, *è da cápo*.

It is not until the evening of the fifth day that he reaches his own paddock fence. His entry is not attended with much *fanfare*. He dismounts, lets down the rails, and rides up to the head station. All is as still as the grave and the door locked. He cooies, a coo-ee comes in reply, and shortly afterwards the overseer makes his appearance with

the keys of the house, the door is opened, and
Mr. Squatter is at home. "Home is home, be it
never so homely," and well it is that it should be
so, for a homelier home than our friend's no man
could possibly desire.

The house, which is constructed of slabs of
iron-bark wood, so roughly put together that
daylight can be seen through the joints, consists of a sitting-room and two bedrooms, all on
the ground floor, there being no upstairs to the
establishment, with a verandah running front and
rear. The furniture is in perfect harmony with
the building, consisting of a rude board, table, a
wool-stuffed, calico-covered lounge, six wooden
chairs, and a cupboard. Seen by the light of a
station-made candle, the sitting-room does not
present a very cheerful appearance—more com-
fortless it could hardly be—and yet it is neither
better nor worse than are the generality of
"keeping" rooms on up-country stations.

Unless he be a married man, the Australian
squatter seldom cares to expend much money on
his habitation. Tenant at will, not lord of the
soil, the interest he takes in his station depends
solely on the profits it yields him, and if he
invest capital on improvements, they are such as
will be likely to make him some return—woolshed, drafting-yards, or fencing. His object

being to make money and not a home, every
shilling of his capital that bears no interest is in
his eyes a shilling completely thrown away, and
to accelerate the accumulation of his " pile" he
is content to live in a style which would seem
rough to the American backwoodsman.

That the reader may have some idea of the
daily life of an up-country squatter, let us follow
the movements of our friend Mr. Smith, the
new occupant of what shall we call his station ?—
Waddy-waddy from the time he turns out in the
morning until the time he turns in at night.
The work will change with the seasons, but the
daily routine will remain pretty much the same
throughout the year.

It is the month of January, the Australian
midsummer, a season when bed has but few
attractions, and Mr. Smith rises with the sun.
His ablutions completed, he lights his pipe, and,
seating himself on the verandah, patiently awaits
the appearance of the old woman who does for
him. His patience is not put to a very severe
test. The door of an adjacent hut—the kitchen
of the establishment—is shortly opened. Frau
Brandt, broom in hand, hobbles across to the
house, and in another half hour the sitting-room
is swept and watered and breakfast on the
board. The fare, though simple, is far more

sumptuous than on many stations, in that there is both milk and butter—luxuries not always found on the squatter's table, even when his herds number thousands, for to drive in a lot of cows from the paddock morning and evening, and to bail them, up and to milk them, gives a peck of trouble, much more trouble than the butter is worth. And so butter and milk are frequently dispensed with, as are likewise, for the same reason, vegetables of every description and fruit, and the squatter's ordinary fare consists of bread, mutton, and tea, or bread, beef, and tea, as sheep or bullock is slaughtered.

It matters not that flocks of wild fowl frequent the adjacent lagoons, that wonga-wonga and wild turkey are to be found in the scrubs, and bronze pigeons, quail, and cockatoo in the paddock, they are seldom seen on the table. The squatter is rarely a sportsman, and if there chance to be kangaroo-tail soup or a bird for dinner, it is an event to be remembered. We are speaking of far distant stations. On those nearer to civilization, if the cooking be little better, there is more variety in the bill of fare.

Breakfast over, our squatter takes down the keys of the premises, and, after a moment's reflection, selects the one belonging to the store, which he proceeds to open. The said store, in

addition to the supplies of flour, tea, and sugar
required for rations, contains an assortment of
dry goods and fancy articles suited to the
requirements of the hands, for the Australian
squatter is a sort of Hiram Anderson in a small
way, with a fine turn for business. Does Hans
want a dress for his wife, Jem a pair of boots,
Mick a jack-knife? Mr. Squatter is ready to
supply them. Nay, should Ching the Chinaman
require the solace of a little opium, the chances
are that he will find it in the store.

There being no shops in the bush, and therefore no competition, Mr. Squatter can place what
prices he likes on his wares, and he seldom errs
on the side of moderation. When settling day
comes the store-book is produced, Han's, Jem's,
Mick's, and Ching's debit accounts are totted up,
and the sum total deducted from their respective
wages ; and what with tobacco, slops, and one
thing or another, a very tidy sum it generally
proves to be. It is all very well to assure the
emigrant that he will be able to save the whole
of his wages—the statement is not borne out by
facts. Unless Mr. Shepherd go naked, he must
purchase clothing ; to provide himself with
clothing he must apply at the station-store.
Store prices are high, and the goods sold of an
inferior description ; and if by the end of the

year his little account does not amount to twenty-five or thirty per cent. of his earnings he is a thrifty fellow. By the sale of tobacco, slops, and sundries, the squatter generally manages to recoup a portion of the money he has to pay away in wages, and considers himself perfectly justified in so doing. Whether he be so or not is a matter of opinion.

It is only on small stations that the squatter is his own storekeeper, and even then he generally has a deputy, in the shape of a colonial experience young gentleman. On large runs there is a storekeeper, and on those of medium size it is the superintendent or overseer who weighs out the rations and sells the wares. But whoever may be the store-attendant, it is the squatter who appropriates the profits. He takes good care that none of his subordinates shall have a finger in the pie; and the young man who hopes to be able to accumulate considerable sums of money by buying and selling and swopping and chaffering with the station hands, or by the sale of old screws to crawling shepherds, shearers, and such like, as we have seen it asserted he can do, will, it strikes us, find himself somewhat disappointed. Unless the floods should have retarded the arrival of his drays the squatter will have plenty of everything in store, and should any article chance to have run out, the shepherd can wait their arrival. Should it be a horse that is wanted, there are plenty of the squatter's own broken-down nags in the paddock from which to make selection.

Your disinterested squatter, if not so rare as the dodo, is the exception, not the rule; and if trading be Mr. Newchum's forte, he will find his talents completely thrown away in the bush. After having cast an eye over the ledger, examined the sundries laid out on the shelves, and made a mental calculation of the rations remaining in store, Mr. Smith relocks the door of the hut, and wends his way to the stockyard. The horses have been driven in from the paddock, and are standing ready to be saddled for the day's work. Out of the twenty in the yard perhaps eight are in fair working condition—the remainder are, or ought to be, on the sick list— from sore back in the majority of cases. If one-half the horses on a station are fit for work it is as much as is usually expected; and, considering the treatment they get, it is surprising that there should be any, for from the day the station 'oss is first bitted to that of his death it is truly a hard road that he has to travel.

Says Mr. Squatter to his superintendent or

overseer—" Rowels, the horse-breaker, will be
here to-morrow; let the stockman and a couple
of black boys start off first thing in the morning and run in the young horses; we want
some fresh ones ' broke.'" In the early
morning stockman and blackboys ride away as
directed, and towards evening a cloud of dust
and much cracking of whips announce the arrival
of the bush mob, comprising all the cripples,
brood mares, and unbroken horses on the station.
Up jumps Mr. Squatter and hies him to the
yard, where already assembled are Mr. Rowels,
the superintendent, Verdant Newchum, Esq.,
and such unemployed 'ands as are desirous of
assisting at the proceedings. Reeking with
sweat after their gallop, and huddled together
in one corner of the yard, stand the captives.
On the top rail of the fence sit the inquisitors,
both white and black. The members of the
tribunal have descended from their rostrum.
After a careful scrutiny of brands and distinguishing marks, a comparison of memoranda, and an
animated debate, sentence has been delivered as
follows:—One cripple to be shot, two strangers
to be banished from the run, four colts to be
branded and gelded, four young 'osses to be consigned to the tender mercies of Mr. Rowels.
It is the morning of the colts' first initia-

tion into the sorrows of station life. Standing dejectedly by the stockyard rails, his quick ears detect the tramp of coming footsteps, and turning his head in the direction of the sound he espies approaching three individuals— one red and two black—Mr. Rowels, red from the fiery Australian sun and the no less fiery bush whisky, and his two native aides, George and Billy. In his right hand Mr. Rowels carries a long forked stick, from his left arm a coil of rope is suspended, whilst the black boys are laden with bits, rollers, bearing-reins, and other instruments of equine torture. Clambering over the fence, Mr. Rowels at once proceeds to business. He uncoils his rope, passes the noose which is bent on one end of it over the fork of his stick, gives the other end to George, with injunctions to hold on like winkin', plants himself firmly within six or eight yards of the fence, tells Billy to round up the colt, and watches. Frightened at the approach of the black boy who has been sent to round him up, the colt tries to effect his escape to the further end of the yard by its unguarded side. But Billy is too smart for him. He gets between him and the rails, and after one or two doubles succeeds in driving him past the spot where Mr. Rowels, stick in hand, is stationed. That worthy

watches his opportunity, and as the poor brute
dashes between him and the railings he dex-
terously slips the noose over his head, and,
dropping the stick, seizes the fall of the rope
with both hands. In a second the slack is paid
out, there comes a sudden jerk, and colt, colt-
roper, and black boys, are all lying in the dust
of the arena. The bipeds are on their feet in a
twinkling; not so the colt. Every time he
attempts to rise, a long pull and a strong pull
and a pull altogether brings him to his knees
again, until, exhausted by his own exertions, and
half throttled by the rope, he lies quivering in
every limb, at the mercy of his captors. Cau-
tiously Mr. Rowels approaches the spot where
he lies, and with a skill only to be acquired by
constant practice, forces a heavy bit between his
jaws, motioning at the same time to one of the
boys to come and stand by him. Everything
being in readiness, Mr. Rowels gently loosens
the noose and draws back a pace or two, when
the colt, finding the pressure on his windpipe
removed, struggles to his feet. Vain, however,
are his endeavours to shake off the black boys
who are now hanging on to the bridle; they are
not to be shaken off. With the same dexterity
which he exhibited in slipping on the bridle Mr.
Rowels now proceeds to buckle on a roller, to the

rings in which he makes fast the reins, and then,
with the additional aid of a stout halter, fastens
his charge to the stockyard fence, where he is
left to champ his bit at leisure; and so the colt
is bitted. In accustoming him to the feel of a
saddle and the weight of a rider similar tactics
are used. It is brute force against brute force,
and the two-legged brute has the best of it.
Despite the most desperate bucking, rearing, and
plunging, the rough-rider manages to stick to
the pig-skin, and the colt finding all his efforts
to dislodge him unavailing, sulkily gives up the
contest and stands stock still. Then comes a
sharp application of the spur, then more rearings
and buckings, then a stubborn refusal to advance,
then another reminder, and so the work of break-
ing continues, to-day Mr. Rowels up, to-morrow
a black boy, until such time as the poor brute
having no longer a kick left in him, and as indifferent to the crack of a stock-whip as he would be to
the report of an eighteen-pounder, is handed over
to the squatter as a "thoroughly broken 'oss"—
broken, if not quite free from vice. So long as he is
kept constantly at work he behaves decently
enough; but let him have a few weeks' spell, let him
discover that he has a new chum or an indifferent
rider on his back, and he will be at his own tricks
again for certain. He is worse than vicious, he is

unreliable. One day he goes like a lamb, another he will buck as if possessed of a devil. But whatever may be his shortcomings he is made to suffer for them. On no more nourishing food than bush grass he is forced to perform journeys that would gruel the oat-fed English roadster. The luxury of clean straw and a warm stable is unknown to him. However hot and tired he may be after his day's work his quarters are the paddock, or, should his master be camped out, he is forced to graze with his legs hobbled. Neither brush nor curry-comb approach his hide, a roll on the ground and a self-administered rubbing against a gum tree are his only cleansings. From badly-stuffed saddles and sweat-hardened saddle-cloths he is a martyr to sore back, and if he escape being hipped or otherwise injured when driven full gallop through the stockyard rails, or gored when in pursuit of wild cattle, he is fortu-nate. Were an English horse to receive the same treatment he would be foundered as a five-year-old. He grunts and bears it; and if a rum 'un to look at he is a good 'un to go—that is, when he can be made to go straight, which, owing to his bringings up is not always. So much has been written on the subject of the marvellous performances of Australian buck-jumpers that little remains to be added. There is, however, one piece of advice that we offer the reader—if he desire to witness the said performances let it be from *terra firma*, not from the brute's back.

With ordinary care and attention one half the horses usually considered necessary for station use might be made to suffice. It is a large station where forty would be required. On one of medium size twenty, exclusive of brood mares and young 'uns, should be ample. Say three for the squatter's own use, the same for superintendent and overseer, and four for the ration carriers, leaving seven unemployed; but then grass-fed horses require a spell occasionally. On stations where the cattle are sufficiently numerous to warrant the employment of regular stockmen, where there is a quiet mob to tail, where there are two or more colonial experience young gentlemen, or where draft-horses take the place of bullocks in hauling fencing, building materials, &c., a few more would of course be requisite.

Having examined his stud, dressed a sore back or two, and given orders to the attendant black boy to saddle Jack or Jerry and turn the others into the paddock, our squatter's morning inspection is over, and he returns to the house. There is no imported stock to scrutinize, no well kept stables to visit, no garden wherein to while away an hour.

The stock at the head station consists of a couple of milch cows, sixteen or twenty working bullocks, and a small flock of rams; the only buildings are the house, kitchen, store, woolshed, and the huts of the overseer, bullock-drivers, and head station hands. It is only on model stations, such as Y——, that the squatter can at all seasons find employment in the vicinity of head-quarters. On distant runs shearing is the only busy time at the head station.

Mounting his horse Mr. Smith rides off through the bush. To-day he is going to visit a flock of sheep pasturing eight miles to the northward; to-morrow he will inspect another flock six miles away in the opposite direction; and so on until every flock on the station has been passed in review, when he will begin again— for being his own manager he is obliged to keep the overseer up to the mark, and see with his own eyes that the station work is properly conducted.

For the first half-hour his road lies through a thinly timbered, well grassed country, or a country that would be well grassed were it not the dry season, and the ground bare and brown as a worn-out carpet. If a splendid country in the eyes of the squatter, whose only thoughts are of his flocks and herds, it would not be so in those of the traveller in search of the picturesque. A dead level of a burnt-sienna hue, dotted with scanty-foliaged, sad-coloured gum-trees; it is about as picturesque as an American fire-barren. It is not at midsummer that the Australian bush resembles an English park, nor does it ever do so, unless it be by moonlight. During the rainy season and early summer the grass may be of as bright a green as in Britain, it can't well be greener; but where are the feathering beeches, the elms, and the oaks, and the chestnuts ?˙

As our friend advances the country becomes more broken and wooded. The run is intersected by deep gullies, the land rises into ridges and hummocks, iron-bark and myall take the place of the blue gum-trees of the plain. It is to this portion of the run that the shepherds drive their flocks when the low lands are flooded, as flooded they very often are in the rainy season—for in Australia there is no wretched compromise between rain and sunshine as in England. When it rains it rains to some purpose—when it is dry it is dry with a vengeance.

Once again the aspect of the run changes. On emerging from a scrubby tract of country our squatter sees before him a wide treeless plain,

bordered by dense thickets, the noontide retreat
of numerous herds of wild cattle ; and at the
further extremity of this plain is situated, we
shall suppose, the hut to which he is bound ; for
having now accompanied him over the three
descriptions of country of which his and most
other runs are composed it is useless to proceed
any further. The bush is the bush, and the
downs are the downs, and it is only in the
vicinity of the various ranges by which the
continent is intersected that there is any scenery
worthy of description.

Arrived at the hut, Mr. Smith dismounts to
get a pannikin of cold tea, and to inquire of the
shepherd's wife the direction in which the sheep
have been headed. The hut, although of the
usual "elevation," is cleaner and neater than are
the generality of shepherds' huts, the present
mistress thereof hailing from Rhineland, and,
like most of her countrywomen, a good *hausfrau*.
Anything more resembling a pigstie than the
ordinary "humpy" of an Australian shepherd it
would be difficult to conceive—a pigstie with
the addition of fleas and vermin of every description. The log cabin of the American backwoodsman if rude of construction is warm and
snug. The interstices between the logs are
caulked with moss ; doors and windows are air-

tight; the roof is water-tight; the floor boarded; and there is a stove with an oven, in which he can bake his bread.

The hut of the Australian shepherd, on the contrary, is seldom impervious to wind and water. Were it not for the honour of the thing the door might be dispensed with. Stove there is none. His furniture consists of a rude bunk, a slab table, and a couple of stools. His cooking utensils are an iron pot, a frying-pan, and a tin pannikin. It is at the camp fire outside his hut that he boils his salt-junk or fries his mutton, and in its embers that he bakes his damper—the bush substitute for bread. His is the life of a savage without the freedom. At daylight each morning he turns out of his lair, and drives his flock from their fold, breakfasts, lights his pipe, and, accompanied by his cur, slowly follows them. And hour after hour he plods in their wake, casting an eye along them from time to time to assure himself that there are no stragglers; amusing himself the while as best he can, generally by hunting the sly opossum, with a view to becoming the happy possessor of a 'possum skin rug. Shortly after midday he heads his sheep for home, arrives at his hut by sundown, and immediately after supper turns in. And so it goes on from day to day, from week to week, from month to month, and not unfrequently from year to year; for when Mr. Shepherd takes his holiday it is rarely that he can resist the temptation of a nobbler, and what becomes of him when he begins to "nobblerize" we have already explained to the reader.

And this is the sort of life that hundreds—shall we say thousands?—of well-educated young men are now leading at the Antipodes—this the employment that Mr. Newchum, who is "so difficult to please," is forced to accept to save himself from starvation, and for not "sticking" to which his friends at home blame him.

His snack finished, our squatter remounts his horse, and canters off in the direction pointed out by Mrs. Fritz as that taken by her husband in the morning, and soon descries that gentleman, with his flock spread out before him.

"Well! And how is he getting along?"

"Oh, pretty gut."

"Not lost any sheep?"

"No. Der oversheer vas town ter tay bevor gestertays, and count him all right. Plenty tincoes about doo."

"Why doesn't he lay poison?"

"So he toes. Killed doo-dree last veeks, but some rascal doo tam smart," &c. &c.

Fritz being a careful shepherd, and his flock in first-rate condition, his master, after talking sheep with him for a few minutes, and telling him to mind and lay plenty of poison for the "tincoes," rides off.

It is not always, however, that the shepherd has as good an account to give of himself as old Fritz, and the answer to "How are you getting along?" instead of being "Pretty gut," is "Very bad." Some sheep have died or been killed by dingoes, or have strayed; nay, not unfrequently the shepherd presents himself at the head station with a long face and a still longer story, the gist of which is that he has had the misfortune to lose half his flock, and wants some one to come help find them. Just imagine poor Mr. Newchum's state of mind on discovering that he has lost a few hundred sheep, for which he is held responsible. The colonel who has had the misfortune to lose a wing of his regiment is a happy man by comparison, for he knows that he will receive a fair trial, and that if not guilty of negligence he will be honourably acquitted. But no such consolation has poor Mr. Newchum in his adversity. That he has lost his sheep will be quite sufficient to condemn him in the eyes of the squatter, his master. And yet in a broken, scrubby country nothing is easier than to lose sheep. The oldest and most careful shepherd may find a squad missing, and whilst searching

for it, lose another. But then when an old shepherd loses sheep his mischance is purely acci-
dental. You don't catch him napping. With
Mr. Newchum the case is different. It can't
possibly have been the result of accident; it is
owing to his infernal laziness and stupidity. He
will be cursed as a stupid, lazy, good-for-nothing
hound, and be sent about his business. If that
were all it would be nothing; but where to find
another situation? Ten thousand miles away
from home, and not a single friend in the colony
to whom he can apply for assistance. Poor
Chummy!

On his road homewards our squatter is over-
taken by his overseer, who has been visiting an
out-station, at the extreme end of the run,
three miles or more beyond where Fritz is
shepherding. A hard-worked man is the same
overseer. It being his duty to count the sheep,
he has to be in the saddle at peep of day, for
many of the huts lie miles away from the head
station, and the counting must be done, as the
sheep leave the fold in the morning or when they
re-enter it at night. On his return home he gets
his snack, saddles a fresh horse, and starts off
again on his visiting rounds; or should his work
a-field be finished for the day, he makes himself
useful about the head station. Where there is a

manager, the overseer is station sergeant-major—
where there is no manager, sergeant-major and
adjutant combined; for not only is he responsible
for the setting-up, so to speak, of the men, but it
is his duty to keep the muster-rolls and draw up
the monthly reports for his commandant's the
squatter's inspection. A very civil smooth spoken
man is Mr. Smith's overseer; for like most of his
class he hopes some day to "squatterize" on his own
account, and has an eye to being allowed to graze
a thousand sheep or so on the run, if he give
satisfaction. And what has the overseer been
doing.

Starting at daybreak, he rode off to *One Tree
Hill* and counted Tom's sheep. Three dead!
Two killed by dingoes, one died when on the
feed. Flock in fair condition, but feed running
short. Thinks it would be well to move him to
Myall Flat next week. Plenty of feed there.
From *One Tree Hill* rode on to *Dead Horse Gully*,
where Dick (Richard Newchum, Esquire) is shepherding. Doesn't think it will answer to keep
Dick—a very careless shepherd. Sheep in
wretched condition, and unable to account for
five. Master Dick too much occupied in 'possum
or paddy-mellon hunting to look after them, &c.

It is seldom that manager or overseer have a
good word to say for Mr. Newchum, unless he be

a colonial experience young gentleman, with plenty of money. No better fun for them than to "put a spoke in his wheel" by sending him to shepherd on some scrubby portion of the run where Argus would have lost his charge, or by persuading him to ride some infernal buck-jumper that no one on the station has been able to sit. His sheep strayed, his steed bolted, down comes Mr. Squatter on him like a shot. Confound his carelessness—curse his stupidity, &c.

Until the paddock fence is reached, the conversation of master and man runs in the same groove. It is of sheep and shepherds, of feed and water, of wool, hides, and tallow. There is but one topic of interest to your genuine squatter —sheep; all the rest is leather and prunella.

At the house awaiting Mr. Smith's return is the stockman of Wilson Brothers, the owners of *Gumbo*, the run adjoining Waddy-waddy. He has been sent over to say that there will be a cattle-mustering at Gumbo on the morrow, and that he, Mr. Smith, would do well to send a man to assist at the drafting, in order to claim any Waddy-waddy cattle running with the Gumbo herd. Cattle-mustering being to the Australian squatter pretty much what a run with the hounds is to the English farmer, Mr. Smith signifies his intention of taking an active part in the proceedings.   He will be at Gumbo in the morning, and will bring with him his acting stockman and a black boy.

For the next few hours our squatter is at a loose end, and endeavours to pass away the time by looking over his accounts, reading an old newspaper, or in smoking his everlasting pipe. Towards sundown he loads his gun and walks over to the stockyard.   Meat is wanted, and there being no regular butcher on the station, he is going to "down" a bullock.   As there are a dozen beasts inside the rails, it will naturally be supposed that his only difficulty will lay in making a selection.   But it is not so.   Our friend's greatest difficulty lies not in the selection of a beast, but in being able to hit him in the right spot when he is selected, more especially in avoiding making a carrom—killing two beasts instead of one with his bullet.   We have seen five shots fired at an unfortunate beast before he succumbed ; whilst more than once the marksman, after resting his gun on the rail and taking aim with all the deliberation of a *Leather-stocking*, has lodged his bullet in the flank of some wretched bag-o'-bones crossing the line of fire, instead of in the fat bullock for whose head it was destined.

. With the slaughter of the bullock the day's

work comes to a termination, and after eating his supper our squatter turns in. There is nothing to keep him up. The overseer, although a very worthy man, is not particularly companionable, and besides he is tired after his day's work and wants to sleep, as do all the other hands on the station. Sitting up by oneself is somewhat slow, more especially when one has no more entertaining reading than a colonial newspaper, or a novel which has been read and re-read a score of times. Much pleasanter between the sheets, and to bed he goes accordingly. Even when there is a manager the squatter's evenings are not often enlivened by his agreeable society, for Mr. Manager, having to be up with the sun, retires early. We are speaking of up-country stations. When the station lies near one of the branch lines of travel—roads they can scarcely be called—there is a constant succession of visitors—squatters going up or down, who make your house their hostel.

Seated on his verandah in the cool of the evening, the squatter sees a horseman approaching, and a single glance is sufficient to tell him that it is a brother squatter, coming, after the manner of the bush, to pass the night. The chances are that he knows him, but whether he does or not he is welcome. Pulling up at a

Q 2

little distance from the house the rider dismounts, unsaddles and unbridles his horse, and turns him into the paddock, and then, with saddle on his shoulder and bridle slung over his arm, walks straight up to where Mr. Smith, or whatever his name may be, is seated. There is not much *empressement* on either side—squatters are not a very demonstrative race. It is " Good evening, Jones."

" Good evening, Smith."

" Going down ?"

" Yes."

" Like to have a wash before supper ?"

" Don't care if I do"—and the formalities of bush reception are over. No more fuss is made with him than there is with the guest at the roadside inn. He has his share of whatever there may be for supper, smokes his pipe, and talks wool with his entertainer until it is time to turn in; gets his breakfast in the morning, and continues on his way, without thinking it necessary to make any apology for having presented himself uninvited. Should Mr. Smith come his way he will be happy to entertain him, and there is an end of the matter.

Did all those demanding hospitality at these " way-stations," as they may be called, belong to the squattocracy, the owners thereof would have

little cause to grumble at the expense of entertaining, such entertainment being on the re-
ciprocity system—*Hodie mihi cras tibi.* But the
squatting fraternity form but a very small percentage of the entertained—the vast majority
consist of "hands" in search of employment. At
some stations the barrack is little better than a
casual ward, and the squatter a relieving officer.

Towards sundown the tramps begin to put in
an appearance. Walking up to wherever the
squatter or manager may happen to be, they
thus address him :—

"Good evening, sir. Do you want any 'ands?"

" No."

" May I stay here to-night?"

" Yes;" which means that he may get his
rations and sleep in some station hut, or in the
woolshed.

What the tax amounts to when there are
a dozen or more casuals to ration, evening after
evening, we leave the reader to imagine. Tax it
is; for although the squatter is not by law compelled to feed and harbour every tramp who
presents himself, he would gain nothing by
refusing to do so, for what was saved in rations
would be more than counterbalanced by the
damage done, out of spite, to the fencing and
other unguarded property on his run. So great

is the tramp nuisance in some parts of the colony that it ought almost to reconcile the pioneer squatter to his solitude.

Whilst Mr. Smith is in the land of dreams let us endeavour to describe the existence that his wife would lead, supposing that instead of being a bachelor he happened to be a married man. In that case the house would be larger and better furnished. There would be a small library, perhaps a piano, although how to get it tuned would be a problem. A servant she would have of course; but there being a constant demand in the towns for good servants, and smart girls having a decided objection to the bush, the said servant is in all probability some old crone, having as much knowledge of household duties as a Tonga islander. If Mrs. Smith could not content herself with bush fare she would have to do her own cooking—and her own clear-starching and ironing into the bargain, if particular as to her linen. Doing one's own work being a mere bagatelle in comparison to having to see that others do it properly, her time would be occupied in looking after her handmaid or handmaidens. Her only recreation would be riding out with her husband occasionally, in reading, or in tending her flower-garden if she have one.

Society she would have next to none. Squatters' wives, although possessed of many admirable qualities, are not as a rule the stamp of women whose society would be cultivated by a lady of refinement; and the only visitors at the station would be the squatters themselves, who, with very few exceptions, are more at home in the stockyard than in the drawing-room, and who prefer talking wool with the host to chit-chatting with the hostess. She would not even have the society of her children; for dreading lest they should develop into gawky currency lads, or still gawkier currency lasses, they have been sent to school, and do not come home for the holidays. The conversation of bullock-drivers and shepherds is not particularly refined; and there are better duennas than the wives of stockmen. Once every two years or so, rarely oftener—for except to your colonial-bred woman, a couple of hundred miles of bush travel is somewhat of an undertaking—she visits the capital. How she diverts herself when there it would be difficult to say, for the shopping of an up-country squatter's wife is soon done, and until the evening little is going on in the shape of amusement.

Melbourne and Sydney are wonderful cities for their age, but they have more attractions for the

money-maker than for the holiday-maker. St.
Kilda and Botany are capital places for "inhal-
ing the briny," but they are hardly as gay as
Newport or Niagara. Brisbane has still fewer
attractions. It is about as lively as a Scotch
town on the Sabbath. It is only a bedlamite
like George Francis Train who could exclaim, "Of
all the cities in the world give me Melbourne!"

Before deciding to try sheep-farming on a distant run the married man would do well to ask
himself the question, "How will my wife adapt
herself to such an existence?—will she be able to
endure it for fifteen or twenty years?" And if there
be the slightest doubt in his mind as to her ability
to do so he would be mad to make the experiment. We know how prone men are to "look
always at the sunny side," to give credence to those
who represent things as they would wish them to
be, and to regard as pessimists those who show
them the reverse side of the picture. Right well are
we aware that the writer who sticks to facts, who
never allows himself to be carried away on the
wings of imagination, is not the one who has the
greatest number of believers—that the more improbable the tale the greater the interest. But
we prefer being regarded as a pessimist by the
. inexperienced to being anathematized as a lying
optimist by those who, guided by our representa-

tions, have been led astray ; and we again plainly tell the reader that life on a remote run is about the very dreariest existence that a man could possibly select—drearier and lonelier than that of the settler in a small township in Canada or the United States. And if it be dreary to the man whose heart is in his work, and who from sunrise to sunset is riding about his run inspecting his sheep and talking to his shepherds, what must it be to the well-bred woman who, with no better companion than an ignorant servant, is obliged to remain at home the livelong day, and whose only visitors, from year's end to year's end, are squatters—men who, whatever may be their sterling worth, are in most instances very far from being what is known as " presentable."

Clearings life is not particularly lively, but in comparison to that led by the wife of an Australian squatter it is as May Fair to the Hebrides. Should the settler's wife be too genteel to visit the Heffernans and O'Gradys, her neighbours, she can associate with the parson's wife and the lawyer's wife and the doctor's wife, without loss of caste. On Sunday she can attend church or meeting, and visit from time to time the nearest city or watering-place—for it must be indeed a remote township where there is neither rail nor water communication within a distance of fifteen or twenty miles. If out of the world she is not so far removed from it as to be unable to hear its pulsation.

The squatter's wife, on the contrary, has neither parson's wife, nor lawyer's wife, nor doctor's wife with whom to exchange an idea. Parson, lawyer, doctor, live in some township a hundred miles away, and the nearest church is in the same locality. Unless she choose to "assist" at a native "corrobbery," or to invite the wives of the bullock-drivers and stockmen to tea, she may keep her toilettes locked up in her wardrobe until her next visit to the capital, or until such time as her husband having made his pile, they shall—oh, happy day!—return to Europe and civilization.

Accompanied by his stockman and a lynx-eyed black boy, Mr. Smith rides over to Gumbo to assist at the cattle-mustering, according to promise. The day is still young when he arrives at the head station, but, as nothing can be done until the evening, he turns his horse into the paddock, and smokes and talks wool, and talks wool and smokes, until it is time to be moving. About four o'clock the horses are driven into the stockyard and saddled, and half an hour later eight well-mounted men ride through the paddock rails. An hour's riding brings them to the

spot selected for the first drive—a plain of
perhaps six hundred acres in extent—where they
find the quiet mob or "coachers" quietly grazing
under the watchful care of a stockman and a
couple of black boys. And what's the news?

The news is sufficiently satisfactory. There is
a large mob of wild cattle in the scrub on the
further side of the plain, and as it is about feeding time, the black boy, who has been sent out
to reconnoitre, may be expected back in half an
hour or so, with the intelligence that the said
mob is in motion. About the time specified
the black scout makes his appearance. The wild
cattle have left the scrub, and are feeding in the
direction of the quiet herd now in the centre of
the open. It is high time to commence operations.

Leaving a couple of men *en vidette*, the remainder of the party start off for the opposite
side of the plain, making a wide *détour* to escape
detection. A quarter of an hour's riding brings
them to the edge of the scrub which the wild
cattle have so recently quitted. There is a
moment's halt, a hurried consultation, and then
the word " off" is given. In an instant the
horsemen are bearing down full gallop on the
unsuspecting herd. Another twenty seconds
and they will be amongst them. It is two to

one on the pursuers—when up go fifty heads, ditto fifty tails, and away they all dash in a cloud of dust across the open. The odds are now the other way. The pursued have a good start, they have avoided the coachers, and have only a short half mile to cover to reach the timber on the opposite side of the plain, where they will be in comparative safety. The distance has been diminished one-half—another four hundred yards and they will have reached the timber—when, just in the nick of time, out gallop the two black videttes from their hiding place, who, with much shouting and waving of red handkerchiefs, succeed in heading them off in a diagonal direction. So sudden is the wheel made by the herd, that horses less accustomed to the work than those ridden by the leading stockmen would be unable to swerve in time to avoid a collision. But Australian stock-horses can twist and double in a manner truly marvellous. They wheel sharply to the left, pass in rear of the herd, and are on the near flank in a twinkling.

Cut off from the scrub on that side of the plain, the fugitives now make a bold dash for their late quarters at the other extremity. But before they are half way across, they are headed off again, and, after one or two doubles, are driven into the ranks of the quiet mob. Vain are their attempts to escape. Round and round the united herds gallop the "musterers"—stockmen swearing and cracking their whips, black boys yelling and waving their handkerchiefs. It is as exciting as a bull-fight, and almost as dangerous; for when his "dander is riz," Australian toro is not a whit less savage than his Andalusian brother.

Watch that short-horned, curly-crested, red bull, pawing the ground yonder. Twice within the last five minutes has he received a taste of Frank's stock-whip. His blood's up, and he means mischief. Charge! There he goes, full tilt at Frank, who is just now looking in another direction. Frank doesn't see him, but his steed does. You can't take him unawares. He knows the feel of a bull's horns, and has no desire to increase his experience. He avoids Master Toro's rush with a quickness that would earn him an ovation in the ring at Seville, wheels in his own length, and canters up on the truant's near side, keeping at just the right distance to enable his rider to use his stock-whip with the most telling effect.

Crack! crack!! crack!!! That last was a stinger. No resisting such forcible arguments as those. Down goes our red friend's tail—round he comes at full speed. Crack! And bellowing with rage and pain, he hides his diminished head in the centre of his fellows.

It is not always, however, that Toro has the worst of it. When the horse is young and unaccustomed to the work, or when the rider is a green hand, having more faith in his own judgment than in his steed's sagacity, the tables are sometimes turned, and instead of there being a bull "rounded in," horse and rider are bowled over. But, all things considered, mishaps of this description are of rare occurrence. The greatest number of casualties arise, not from the charges of savage bulls, but from fallen trees and overhanging branches, which, dangerous at all times, are doubly so at night, when, however bright the moonlight, it is impossible to judge distances with any degree of accuracy.

After half an hour's "ringing," during which time a hundred fruitless attempts at escape have been made by the captives, the word forward is given, and the united herds, watchfully guarded, front, rear, and on either flank, are put in motion and headed for the scene of the next drive, a plain two miles to the westward.

Although quieter, the wild uns are not altogether reconciled to the situation. Ever and anon some unruly member of the herd charges out of the ranks, and endeavours to make a bolt of it. But before he has gone fifty paces, the nearest horseman is alongside him—swish! goes the eight-foot lash of the stock-whip, and back he comes again at score.

Wonderfully expert with the whip are these same Australian stockmen. It is to them what the lasso is to the *gaucho*, and a bush swell of the first water is the expert in the use thereof. The entire mounted contingent of a station—cornstalks, new chums, and black boys are disciples of the art, and do their best to graduate in stock-whip honours, and the bandannas that are yearly torn up for "crackers" on a large cattle run, would suffice to stock a moderate-sized haberdashery. That it is not an accomplishment easily acquired we can testify, for we have made the essay and signally failed—so signally indeed, that we nearly broke our neck in the attempt to master it.

Charmed with the performance of a certain stockman, an ambidextrous individual, who made his whip crack with a report like that of a rifle, and who could with equal certainty flick a fly from the back of a bullock or make the blood spurt, we in an evil hour purchased what may be called his "showing off whip"—a pretty little instrument, with a handle of some fifteen inches, and a lash of nearly as many feet. A working stock-whip, with an eight-foot lash, was not sufficient for us—it must be the "whole hog or none." After a week's practice, during which we used up a score of crackers, and inflicted fully double that number of lashes on different parts of our person, we considered ourselves sufficiently master of the art to go through our performance mounted. If we could crack the whip on foot we must surely be able to do so on horseback, so we saddled a stock horse which we knew to be quiet under fire, and, whip in hand, mounted. The arena chosen for the display of our proficiency was the open space in front of the head station, and assembled on the verandah to witness it were the squatter, our host, his superintendent, and a colonial experience young gentleman—about the greatest muff that ever donned Bedford cords and a cabbage tree hat. Our first appearance in public, we were just a *leetle* flurried, but after settling ourselves well in the saddle, patting the mare encouragingly on the neck, and casting an eye at the house, we began. Up went the arm, round the lash, drop the wrist. O. K— but instead of the anticipated crack, there came a snort of pain from the mare, accompanied by a plunge which deprived us of both stirrups. Buck—buck—buck—third and last time of asking, and

when, having realized an independence, he shall
return to Europe and participate in all the
pleasures of London and Paris. If he bear ill-
will to any one it is to Mr. Richard Newchum,
whom overseer or superintendent has just reported
for divers high crimes and misdemeanors.
Whatever his reveries, he is aroused therefrom
by the thud, thud, thud of a mob of kangaroo.
A view halloa! and the chase begins.

There is the promise of a quick run, for the
dogs are after a flyer, and the ground is as level
as a billiard-table. Now casting a glance over
the right shoulder, now over the left, to have a
look at the situation, the way her ladyship hops
along is a caution to cricket balls. What the
best pace of a kangaroo may be we are unable to
say, but for a short spin over the flat, or, better
still, down a slight incline, we would back one of
our marsupial friends to beat the fleetest deer
that ever trod heather. It is not until a considerable distance has been covered—until there
is a rise in the ground—that the kangaroo
begins to flag; then the dogs gain on her rapidly.
Another two minutes and she will be turned over,
when, just in the nick of time, comes a diversion
in her favour. Right in front of the dogs, and
between them and their prey, out jump another
mob, their rear brought up by a whacking " old

man." The nearest of the ruck, it is to this
gentleman that the dogs now turn their attention,
and although tired with their run, so long as he
keeps his nose up hill they press him closely.
The old fellow is, however, wide awake, and
watching his opportunity, he doubles on his pursuers, and goes tearing down hill at a tremendous
pace—thirty feet at a bound at the lowest calculation. But the dogs are not to be circumvented.
Although losing ground at every stride, they
keep after him, and have him still in view when
he comes to the level. Over the flat they go ding-
dong, the kangaroo some hundred yards in
advance of the hounds, the huntsmen about the
same distance in rear of them. The pace is
nothing like so fast as it was at first go off—
horse and dogs are getting blown, and the old
man is husbanding his energies. Slower and
slower grows the chase. The huntsman comes
up with his hounds. The gallop subsides into
a canter, the canter into a trot, and Master
Kang, seeing his enemies fairly distanced, puts
on a final spurt, and disappears behind a belt of
timber.

Much disgusted, our huntsman dismounts and
proceeds to load and light his pipe—in Australia, as elsewhere, the great consoler in adversity—and with the first half dozen puffs, his

bad humour vanishes. There has been no kill—
but what's the odds? The run was a good one,
and the old rascal deserved to save his tail, he
went so pluckily. What to do next? The dogs
must have a rest before they can again try con-
clusions with the kangaroo, and besides, they
want water. There is a creek half a mile distant—best to make for it. Leading his horse by
the bridle, for the creek he steers accordingly.

It is not often that the Australian squatter is
seen footing it through the bush. His maxim
is never to walk when he can ride, and for nine
months out of the twelve his maxim is a sensible
one. During the hot season walking through
the bush is almost as exhausting as walking
through the desert of Sahara. The heat is intense, the ground like a brick-kiln, there is
little shade, and one may travel miles without
coming to water. The creeks are dried up, the
water-holes few and far between, and the water
in them warm and brackish. Many a time,
when travelling through the burnt-up bush—
giddy from the intense heat, and ready to faint
for want of water—have we flung ourselves alongside a mud-hole and sucked its moisture through
our handkerchief, and right thankful for it,
although it was the colour and consistency of
molasses. Verily a thirsty land during the sum-

mer months is Australia. During the wet season
there is the other extreme. The ground is like
a sponge, the grass long and dank, and a walk
through the bush about as pleasant as a wade
through the Bog of Allan. Deducting nine
months for the hot and rainy seasons there
remain but three, during which a bush-tramp
can be undertaken with any degree of satisfaction. During these three months the bush does,
to a certain extent, present the appearance which
Australians would have us believe that it always presents—that of an English park. But
only to a certain extent. We do not wish to be
hypercritical, but we must say that we think the
vaunted beauty of the Australian bush to be
somewhat overrated. We cheerfully endorse all
statements as to the greenness (in spring) of the
grass, and as to the brilliancy of the flowers.
We admit that the disposition of the trees is
park-like. We will even go so far as to acknowledge that, seen from a distance, the scrubs bear
some resemblance to plantations. But there our
admissions end. We cannot allow that Australian trees are like English trees—that Australian
creeks are like English rivers—that the flowers
are as fragrant as in the old country. And if
the flora of Australia will not bear comparison
with that of the mother country, still less her

fauna. The marsupials cannot be named in the same breath with the ruminants of the old world.

If Master Kang be swift of foot no one can accuse him of beauty—a great overgrown rat, with as much grace in his movements as a giraffe. Wallaby paddy-mellon and kangaroo rat are quarto, octavo, and duodecimo editions of the same animal. Of the great opossum family— ursine opossums, zebra opossums, phalangers, bandicoots, &c.—one variety is uglier than the other. The Australian porcupine, or porcupine anteater, is the most hideous of a species not particularly famed for its beauty. The water-mole—the ornithorhynchus—by Jove, we have split our pen over that word, and fear we have misspelled it after all!—is neither fish, flesh, fowl, nor good red herring. It is like nothing but its own proper self, and ought to be ashamed of the resemblance. The dingo is a brute—half dog, half wolf—but altogether too disreputable for the relationship to be acknowledged by either ancestor. So much for the quadrupeds.

The birds, though gay of plumage, have no voice, or rather no idea of harmony. We can imagine nothing more goose-flesh-making, more teeth-on-edge-setting, than the screaming of a flock of cockatoo, unless it be the hideous chuckle of the laughing jackass.

It is rather in reptiles that Australia comes
out strong. For the erpeologist it is a very
paradise—carpet snakes, black snakes, deaf
adders, and many other varieties, mostly venomous, besides lizards of gigantic proportions. For
our own part we prefer a country where we can
stretch ourselves on the turf and enjoy our siesta
without having a snake to keep us company.
That death from snake-bites are of rare occurrence matters little. That people have been
bitten is quite sufficient to make one feel a " sort
o' scared" when a great black snake goes
gliding away in the grass alongside one, and
to seriously disturb one's slumbers. So at
least it is with us, but men are differently con-
stituted.

Now halting to take stock of the feed (it
wont be as abundant three months hence)—now
to call the dogs, which are lagging, our huntsman leisurely advances.

See! What is that moving through the
bushes down by the creek yonder? The old
man, for a ducat. Yes! it is the old wretch,
sure enough.

Coo-ey! After him good dogs! You'll have
him this bout to a certainty.

Half a mile in the direction he is going the
creek makes a bend, and unless he keeps clear of

it or takes to the water he is a gone kangaroo for sure. He seems to know that the danger is greater than before, for he claps on full steam and widens the gap at every bound. If, instead of keeping that great tiller of his amidships, he would only put it to starboard, he might yet avoid the bend and the unpleasant alternative of having either to swim the creek or run the gauntlet. But no, he goes straight as an arrow. He sees the water in front of him, and gets bewildered. He tries to double. Too late! The dogs are close upon him. He turns to bay. There is a short struggle, and then over he goes, the dogs on top of him. The huntsman rides up, dismounts, gives him a couple of knocks on the head, and poor Kang is at rest, and for ever. Although his pelt could be made into excellent leather—soft as kid, but tough as calf skin—and though there are worse dishes than fillet of kangaroo with sharp sauce, our huntsman contents himself with cutting off the tail—not as a trophy, but that his cook may convert it into soup—kangaroo-tail soup, the great bush dainty. And with the tail at his saddle-bow he rides homewards.

Dingo hunting can hardly be included in our list of bush sports and pastimes. The dingo runs fast and gamely, but he makes such havoc amongst the sheep—is such a blood-stained felon that he is deemed unworthy of meeting his death in any such honourable way, and is destroyed by means of poison.

Where emu are plentiful they are occasionally hunted, but unless one have good dogs emu hunting is a sport in which the runs exceed the kills by a many. After a dozen attempts we certainly succeeded in riding one down, but we did not commence the pursuit until the horse of the man who accompanied us had been thoroughly beaten. Not only have emu speed, but wind. On pulling up after a two miles' gallop we have seen the flock of which we were in pursuit go scurrying across the plain, apparently as fresh as ever. If to kill be the huntsman's aim, his best plan is to rush the mob the instant he sights it, and endeavour to drop one with a revolver. We are presuming that he is mounted. Should he be on foot he will of course use a rifle, and this brings us to the second division of bush sports—shooting.

Bush shooting is much more varied than bush hunting, which is limited to the pursuits of kangaroo and emu. If the sportsman be a good rifle shot, he can stalk kangaroo, wallaby, emu, and black swan; whilst for his smooth-bore there are cockatoo, wonga-wonga, and bronze pigeons, quail, wild turkey, and various descriptions of wild duck.

For the larger game a black boy is the best pointer; the dog may have the finer nose, but the biped has the keenest eye-sight. Nothing escapes him. The flight of a bee suffices to direct him to the spot where the swarm have made their hive; whilst the mark of a claw on a tree-trunk reveals to him where massa 'possum lies secreted. He comes to a point. You strain your eyes, but see nothing. You shake your head negatively. He advances a few paces, points again, grins, and whispers—"wallaby." No wallaby can you descry. Another shake of the head—another advance, and another, and another, and another, until at length you think you can discern, squatting beneath a bush, some hundred paces distant, the outline of something. What that something may be you are unable to determine, for it is perfectly motionless, and in colour differs nothing from the bush in the background. Had your attention not been directed to it, you might have stood for an hour without perceiving even that shadowy outline. As it is you hesitate to fire. But the darky nods encouragingly. You level your rifle, draw a bead—bang! and with a convulsive spring over rolls a wallaby.

If a native pointer be of service when stalk-
ing big game in the open, for scrub shooting he
is absolutely indispensable. Without him one
cannot get along at all. In the scrub he acts
not only as pointer but as guide, and foolhardy •
is the man who ventures into these almost im-
penetrable jungles without him. After a comparatively short apprenticeship the American
hunter will strike a line through the woods with
tolerable accuracy. By observing the slant of the
trees, and the moss on their trunks, he can keep
within a point or two of his true course, or if he
be of a very timid nature, and afraid of trusting
to such signs, he has only to carry a compass
and guide his steps by the needle. But in the
Australian scrubs there is, so far as our experience goes, nothing in the aspect of the trees,
or in the colour of their bark, to guide one, and
the covert is so dense that the shadows thrown
are unreliable. To make anything like a straight
course one must be provided with a compass
and steering by compass is slow work, when,
owing to the obstacles in one's path, necessitat-
ing a twist here and a *détour* there, one has to
stop every few seconds to consult it, and do some
mental dead reckoning. With a black boy as
guide, one is as safe in the scrub as in the open.
No danger of his losing his way. His senses

have been sharpened by that best of whetstones, necessity; he knows the ropes as well, perhaps better, than the *fera natura* of which he is in search. All you have to do is to follow him; avoid as far as possible leaving your dry-goods hanging on the bushes, and pot the wild turkey when he points them out.

For wild fowl shooting a retriever or water spaniel would doubtless be of service, as likewise a brace of setters for quail and pigeon. But it would scarcely answer for the squatter to keep a regular kennel, and very fair sport can be had without one.

Of the fishing nothing need be said. We don't care for ground fishing, and the fly fishing is beneath contempt.

The last four months of the year are the busiest and pleasantest, for it is the Australian spring—the season of lambing and shearing— and last, not least, the one which immediately precedes our squatter's yearly visit to the capital. The lambing season is heralded by the appearance of numerous little detachments of that got-no-work-to-do tribe of which mention has already been made—a tribe which, notwithstanding the alleged insufficiency of labour in the colonies, somehow or another musters strong. Now is their harvest, now the time when they may feel certain of being able to obtain employment, and a fair day's wage for a fair day's work. For the last six months, or since the termination of shearing, the usual answer to their stereotyped demand, " Do you want any hands?" has been "No." Now it is "Yes," for extra labour is required for lambing and washing and shearing.

A most remarkable body of men are these same station supernumeraries. Recruited from all classes of society, there are few amongst them from whose story some passage might not be taken by the romance writer to enthral, to entrance, to spell-bind—we forget the correct expression—the most exacting of sensational novel readers. From their personal experiences he could, with very little trouble, collect sufficient material for a dozen "Nights and Mornings," or "Mornings and Nights." "The Australian Nights" would be a very appropriate title for such a work. It could be written in the same style as those thousand and one of Arabia, which charmed our boyish fancies ; but instead of the stories being narrated by a pretty odalisque at the bedside of an Eastern king, they would be told by a party of casuals huddled together on the floor of a woolshed. As a set-off against " The

Foundling's Story," "The Garroter's Story," "The Burglar's Story," "The Area Sneak's Story," and "The Cadger's Story," there would be "The Young Patrician's Story," "The Captain's Story," "The Parson's Story," "The Lawyer's Story," and "The Doctor's Story," for without overstepping the limits of probability, the peerage and all the liberal professions might be supposed to have their representatives on that woolshed floor. In a country where the scion of a ducal house becomes the pensioner of an innkeeper, the heir-apparent of a viscounty turns bullock-driver, the ex-captain of hussars chores for a party of coarse brutal diggers, the Oxford M.A. breaks stones on the highway, and the LL.B. keeps hut, nothing is improbable, the only difficulty would be in collecting the different characters under one roof-tree—difficult, but far from impossible. On one station that we visited the storekeeper was a baronet's eldest son, the ration-carrier an ex-lieutenant of dragoons, and the tailer of the quiet mob a young gentleman who had served in the navy, whilst the squatter, the master of all three, was an individual who could barely sign his own name, and whose manners were on a par with his education. "Nothing derogatory in honest labour" will doubtless exclaim many a father who has a son in the colonies sowing his wild oats. There is not ; it is certainly not pleasant to be bullied and badgered by a boor, and to be treated as a servant by a man who in every respect save wealth is one's inferior, but that there is nothing degrading in honest labour we admit. But— for there is a but, and a very important one—but supposing that a man can find no work, or that the employment offered him is beyond his strength—what then? He can either hang himself or wander to and fro in the land, getting a night's lodging here, a day's work there—become not an amateur casual, but a casual perforce. Once on the tramp he may be accounted a lost man. Forced to associate with some of the greatest ruffians unhung, he soon becomes such an one as themselves. He grows callous, loses all relf-respect, and instead of a reformed character he develops into the blackest of black sheep. No man would, we presume, have the hardihood to assert that the proper way to reform a prodigal is by sending him to live with beings more wicked than himself, and yet that is just the course that some parents adopt with their wayward sons. They pack them off to Australia, the country where, in proportion to the size of the flock, there are more black sheep than in any other. The excuse that in Australia a man is forced to work in order to live, and that labour is purifying and ennobling, is a very lame one. Australia is not the only country where the impecunious have to work for their daily bread, where labour purifies, &c. The same can be said of all countries. Then why select Australia? We again assert, without fear of contradiction, that in no country is the descent to Avernus easier than in Australia, none where the road to amendment is narrower and more rugged. Those who pretend that the demand for labour is always in excess of the supply, that no man who is willing to work need be idle, assert what is not the fact. Except at the busy seasons—lambing, shearing, harvesting—the supply of unskilled hands exceeds the demand, and for six months out of the twelve there are hundreds, ay, thousands of men, scouring the country in every direction, seeking work and finding none. As may be imagined, a large proportion of them belong to the white-handed class—unfortunates who, having been brought up to no trade and physically unfitted for the heavier labours of the farm, apply in vain for permanent employment. They must be content to take any odd jobs that turn up, and to perform the work that Hodge and Mick think beneath them. That the gentleman by birth and education should be so reduced as to be forced to accept with gratitude the odd jobs declined by hinds and ploughmen, is, however, a mere nothing in comparison with the degradation of being obliged to live on terms of equality with the wretches who form the left subdivision of the body casual—the sweepings and the off-scourings of humanity. There's the rub. It is not the work that degrades, but the association, and could the parent who so sternly refuses to entertain poor prodigal's petition that he may be furnished with the means to return home and given one more trial —be only transported by some good *Diable Boiteux* to the woolshed or barrack of an Australian sheep station, and permitted to listen for an hour or two to the conversation of the casuals therein assembled, he would, unless he were a very hard-hearted parent indeed, proceed to kill the fatted calf without a moment's delay. To save his son from such companionship no sacrifice would seem too great.

Few spare moments has the squatter now. He is up and away before sunrise, and seldom returns until after dark. If he is wanted he must be sought at the lambing stations, for there

there was an empty saddle, and a man lying insensible on the ground. Needless to say that we were that unfortunate. When we came round we found ourselves on our bed, Mr. Squatter at our head, Mr. Superintendent at our feet, and Mr. Newchum, who professed to understand surgery, punching away in the region of our hump ribs, in the hopes of being able to discover some broken bone, or dislocated member whereon to operate. In this he was disappointed. No bones were broken, but we felt as if we had just been released from the loving embraces of the "Scavenger's Daughter." On making inquiries as to the cause of the mishap, we learnt that we had managed in some way or another to bring the swell of the lash right under the mare's tail, and that she, naturally objecting to stock-whip in that fashion, "had bucked us off." Weeks elapsed before we renewed the experiment, and when we did so the length of the lash was curtailed one half—we carefully eschewed all flourishes and fancy work, and went to work in the "Gee-up, Dobbin" style, befitting a Newchum and Old Country man.

Slowly and silently the mustering party advances. No more shouting and cracking of stock-whips, for wild cattle have quick ears, and once stampeded pursuit is hopeless.

At the expiration of an hour a halt is made, and the black boys are sent forward to reconnoitre. The moon has now risen, and, seen by her light, the dreary monotonous bush looks if not precisely like "some noble English park," much more winsome than it did in the glare of noonday. The *coup d'œil* is indeed eminently picturesque. Of all Australian scenes, cattle mustering by moonlight is perhaps the one which to the stranger is at the same time the most novel and the most fascinating. The open forest, the surging, closely-wedged herd of party-coloured cattle, the mustering party on their hollow flanked steeds, the whole lighted up by a bright Australian moon, form a picture which must be seen to be thoroughly appreciated. The bush, like Melrose, to be seen aright must be visited by "pale moonlight"—the colouring is too subdued for the garish light of day.

The halt is not of very long duration. In a few minutes the black boys return with the intelligence that the mob of which they have been in quest is now feeding in a thinly timbered tract of country half a mile off, and not on the plain, as was expected. Again there is a hurried consultation, and then the gang is told off into two equal divisions, one of which rides away to the front, the other remaining behind to guard the

prisoners. Mr. Smith belonging to the latter
division, we will take up our position beside him.
Five minutes have elapsed, and nothing has
occurred worthy of comment. Once or twice a
charge has been made by some recalcitrant bull
or bullock, but he has been pursued and driven
back again in less than no time. Not a sound
is heard but the lowing of the captives, and an
occasional " Look out, Bill," " Mind yer eye,
Tom," from some watchful member of the party,
who thinks he discerns a head lowered prepara-
tory to an attempt at evasion.

Ten minutes gone and no change in the situation. In the foreground a surging sea of glis-
tening hides and horns, with six wild-looking
horsemen flitting around it; in the background
the moonlit forest. Hark! What was that?
A shout, surely! Yes, there it is again. The
sentinels hear it—there is a cry of " Here they
are," and a general tightening of reins and
settling into saddles. Nearer and nearer come
the sounds. The heavy tramp of many hoofs
can be distinctly heard, and the sentries think it
high time to look out for number one—to stand
the charge of fifty or a hundred head of wild
cattle not being in the night's programme.
Giving the herd a final ringing, they retire in a
body to the rear, and hardly have they taken up

their positions ere the leaders of the wild mob are seen coming at lightning speed through the timber. A short interval, and then the main body comes thundering along, followed by the stragglers, and, last of all, *ventre à terre*, gallop the mustering party. Owing to the timber and to the broken nature of the ground, this mob is not as compact as that first mustered, and some score beasts have managed to outflank the enemy. In a cloud of dust, and with tremendous impetus, the main body bears down on the coachers. There is a violent collision, a great surging of heads and backs, and fifty beasts are added to the number of the mustered. Before the new-comers have time to recover from their surprise at this unexpected rencounter, up gallops the escort, and the ringing recommences with greater energy than ever. Leaving them to their circling and rounding in, let us watch the right sub-division going through their " pursuing practice." It is a pretty sight. The stragglers have formed themselves into half a dozen little squads, and each of them is now being pursued by a stock-man. Doubling in and out of the timber, now wheeling to the right, now to the left, one and all are doing their best to avoid being driven into the ranks of the coachers. To follow the lot being impossible, let us confine our attention to that knot of four of which stockman Frank is the custodian. An experienced stockman is Frank—a better rider never put foot in stirrup. To see him go swinging along there at a hand gallop, one would imagine that the ground was as level as Newmarket racecourse, instead of being broken and full of windfalls. Buck. There goes his horse over a fallen tree, and hardly has he alighted when, twisting round on his hind legs with cat-like agility, he bucks back again, for the runaways have doubled, and as they double he doubles too, without any pull of the bit or pressure of the leg on the part of his rider. If his rider allows himself to be taken unawares, and gets a spill, that's his look out. The man who can't keep his seat as long as his horse can manage to keep his legs, has no business to go cattle-mustering.

Although Frank's horse has not had the advantage of *haute école* training—not been even so much as lunged—he is as supple as any trick-horse at Astley's, and can halt when at full gallop like an old charger.

Look there! Did Bucephalus himself ever stop shorter, and if so where was Alexander? Most men would have found themselves on their steed's neck, perhaps still further removed from their saddle. Frank's seat has not been in the least shaken. He is used to that sort of performance, and habit is everything.

Off they go again at a nice easy canter, keeping just sufficiently in rear of the bullocks to avoid a collision, in case of sudden wheel or double. Now they are hidden by an intervening belt of timber—now they are seen in the bright moonlight, scouring across the open. Down goes Frank's head on his horse's neck. A stumble? No; only an overhanging branch, much too near his head to be pleasant. What with branches above, and stones, holes, and windfalls below, and the trunks of trees on either side of him, the cattle-musterer has not only to keep his weather eye, but both eyes open; and even then accidents will and do happen, and the yearly list of casualties—broken heads and broken bones—is a large one. When fox-hunting has lost its charm, and steeplechasing its excitment, let the *blasé* sportsman pay Australia a visit. If, when going full speed over broken ground after wild cattle, with no stronger light than that of the moon to show him how to steer, his pulse does not beat full ten to the minute faster, his is a hopeless case; for unless it be grizzly bear hunting with bowie-knife instead of rifle and revolver, we can think of no pursuit equally dangerous and exciting.

But here at last comes Frank with his

refractory lot, and the others having been already rounded in, the second drive has been accomplished without mishap of any description. Although two more drives are to be attempted, we shall not accompany the mustering party any further on their moonlight raid. Outline sketches of bush life is all that our space permits—the reader must do his own shading.

Shortly after sunrise the mustering party reach the paddock rails, and coachers and wild cattle are driven pell-mell into the stockyard. Although all hands are pretty well tired out after their night's labours, an hour is all the time that is allowed them to rest and breakfast. At the expiration of that time there is a general move in the direction of the stockyard, and the work of drafting commences.

A heavy cloud of dust hangs over the enclosure, and great is the commotion amongst the three hundred beasts penned therein on catching sight of the drafters. Most of them have been in that yard before, and instinct tells them that these former visits were anything rather than pleasurable. They have an indistinct recollection of being thrown to the ground and tortured in a most cruel way by bipeds very similar in appearance to those now approaching, and they feel nervous—so nervous that were it not for the great height and strength of the stockyard rails they would vamoose the ranche without waiting for a closer inspection.

At one end of the yard is a narrow passage or drafting lane, and communicating with it by means of heavy swing gates are three drafting yards—one for the reception of the "strangers," another for the fat beasts destined for the butcher or the pots, the third for those to be branded or gelded. A stockman having been stationed at each of the three gates giving ingress to the drafting-yards, station bosses and station deputies perch themselves all of a row on the top rail of the fence, and black boy George is told to go at it. At it he goes forthwith. Armed with a stout stick he enters the yard and stealthily approaches the corner in which the beasts are huddled. Thwack comes his shillelah on the back of the nearest bullock—thwack—thwack— thwack. "Well done, George," cries Mr. Squatter from his perch. "Well done, George, that starts 'em." Starts them it does, sure enough, a dozen beasts wheel round and make a rush for the opposite end of the yard, and a short-necked bull charges the darkey, whom he is within an inch of pinning against the railings; but a miss is as good as a mile, and nothing daunted, at it Master George goes again. After much thwacking and pursuing and being pursued, he manages to drive a score or so into the lane leading to the drafting-yards, at the entrance to which he stands sentry.

The first beast to be drafted is a bullock with the Gumbo brand and ear mark, and as he is in prime condition the gate of the fat beast yard is opened by the janitor, and in he goes. Next come a couple of heifers belonging to the Gumbo quiet mob, and as fat beasts and herders have to keep company until the departure of the former for the pots, they go through the same gate as their predecessor. Number four is an unbranded yearling bull, and words run high as to ownership. He is claimed by Wilson Brothers and by the stockmen from two neighbouring stations. But the evidence given by the latter being deemed insufficient to establish a title, and possession being in Australia, as elsewhere, "nine points of the law," he is ultimately, amidst much swearing and protesting, drafted into the yard appropriated to the Gumbo un-branded. And so the work progresses. One after another, fat beasts and herders, the un-branded and the strangers, are driven into their respective pens, and the main yard is empty. The strangers are handed over to the envoy stockmen to be redrafted and driven off to the

stations whence they hail; the quiet mob and
the fat beasts are sent out to graze under the
guardianship of a stockman and two black boys,
and preparations are made for branding. One
lights a fire, another runs for the brands and
tackle, whilst the head stockman sharpens his
knife on a piece of whetstone. Everything is
ready—tackle rove, irons hot, knife sharpened,
and the patients drafted into the operating or
branding-yard.

Much in the same manner that Mr. Rowels
roped his colt, Mr. Stockman proceeds to rope a
calf, only that, in the present instance, there is a
double roping. The victim is lassoed round the
neck, and lassoed round the hind legs; and so
securely fastened to the railings that kicking is
out of the question. Our stockman being an old
practitioner, there is no delay or bungling. The
double operation of cutting and ear-marking is
performed with marvellous rapidity. Up rushes
a grinning black boy with the branding irons;
there is a hissing noise, and a smell of burnt hair
and flesh; the tackle is loosened, and the poor
victim is suffered to make his escape. And so
one after another the beasts are branded, and with
branding the work of mustering is brought to a
termination.

Such, during the first seven or eight months

of the year, is, briefly told, the life of the
ordinary up-country squatter. If a sportsman,
he will keep two or three dogs, and run a
kangaroo occasionally; or, with a black boy as
pointer, beat the nearest scrubs for wild turkey
and wonga-wonga pigeons.

It is not on account of the scarcity of game in
the bush that the squatter is so rarely a sportsman; but rather, we imagine, because he is
always in such a desperate hurry to make his pile
and return to Europe, that he considers every
hour not devoted to station work to be an hour
completely thrown away. At all events, that is
the only explanation we can suggest. Climate can
have nothing to do with it, for in the pursuit of his
favourite pastime the Anglo-Saxon cares neither
for heat nor cold. Let there be only game to kill,
and whether his road lie through jungle or paddy-
field, with the blazing Indian sun overhead, or
through Canadian snow-drifts and windfalls, with
the thermometer below zero, is to him a matter of
perfect indifference. It is only in Australia—in
what is considered a temperate climate—that his
gun reposes in the rack and his hound in the
kennel. There is no doubt that kangaroo hunting
takes it out of the horses, and that scrub shooting
comes rather hard on one's clothes; but he is a
poor sportsman who would be stopped by such

paltry considerations as these. Heaven knows
it is dull enough in the bush without endeavouring to invent excuses for foregoing one of the few
amusements obtainable.

Supposing our squatter to be a sportsman, his
first care will be to procure three or four good
kangaroo dogs. The kangaroo dog belongs to no
particular breed; he is a cross between the English greyhound and the bloodhound-foxhound-
staghound—who shall say? Could he speak, he
would be puzzled to give his own pedigree. He
may be a cross between a Cuban bloodhound and
a dingo, or between a wolf and a greyhound;
so long as he possesses the requisite points he is
a kangaroo dog. He should have size, strength,
speed, and courage; and if from either parent, or
from some paternal or maternal ancestor he has
inherited a nose, it will be one more point in his
favour. To hear Australians speak of their
kangaroo dogs one would be led to suppose that
they were a pure breed, indigenous to the continent, instead of a mongrel lot, bred no one knows
how, and owing their increased size and weight
to climate.

Ask Mr. Squatter to give you the points of a
kangaroo hound, and he will describe to you a
dog half greyhound, half bloodhound, with the
speed of the former and the endurance of the

latter, fawn in colour, and standing upwards of
thirty inches at the shoulder. That is his idea
of a kangaroo hound, and such dogs are occasionally to be met with, but they are much
sought after, and command a very high price.
We are not so difficult to please. So long as a
dog has a good turn of speed, and is not afraid
to tackle a kangaroo, he may, for all we care, be
a cross between a handsaw and a window-
shutter. The best dog we had was a long-haired,
long-legged, long-nosed customer, a cross, we
should guess, between the ghost of an Irish
deerhound and some vagabond lurcher, a dog so
ugly in every respect that he was alive to his
own ugliness, and would sneak about the place,
and hide in out of the way corners until wanted
—our worst, a genuine kangaroo dog, who was
pronounced by every one to be a perfect picture.
Darn his pictur! For every sovereign we gave
for him he did not return us a cent's worth of
sport. "Handsome is that handsome does;"
and in the purchase of kangaroo dogs we
strongly recommend the reader to avoid the
thoroughbred animal. He wont show a bit
more sport than his hard-favoured relative,
whilst, should he be laid open or drowned by an
old man kangaroo, the pecuniary loss will be
considerable.

Kangaroo hunting is not fox hunting, and one need not be a Nimrod to be able to lay on the dogs and ride up to them; but, in order to insure sport, a certain amount of judgment is necessary. Kangaroo are generally found in "mobs," three or more in each, and, when started, they almost invariably divide, some going one way, some another. To cut off from the rest the one most likely to give a good run, and to get all the dogs after him, is not so easy as might be imagined. Unless judiciously handled, the dogs break too, and once fairly off, all the shouting and hallooing in the world wont bring them back again. They will hunt on their own hook until they kill, and will not be seen again until they turn up at the head station.

Kangaroo and dogs once fairly started, it is comparatively plain sailing; for unless another mob of kangaroo chance to cross the track, or to join in the run, which not unfrequently happens where they are numerous, the hounds will do their work without any assistance on the part of the huntsman. All that he has to do is to ride well up to them, for, unless the country be very open, once lost to view, it is no easy matter to find them again.

Although old dogs generally manage to turn over the kangaroo without injury to themselves, young hounds, or those green to the business, are not always so lucky. When the kangaroo turns to bay, with his back to rock, tree, or water-hole, the well-broken hound knows that he means " ugly," and he endeavours to turn his flank and take him in the rear, or else waits until the arrival of his master. The young, un-trained dog, on the contrary, flies straight at his throat, and pays the penalty for his temerity. The kangaroo clasps him with his fore paws, and with one stroke of his hind foot rips him open. A boar's tusk is not more deadly than the claw of an old man kangaroo. One rip suffices to put the biggest hound *hors de combat ;* and unless he be a staunch one, some time will elapse before he can be induced to tackle one again.

The duration of the run depends almost alto-gether on the lie of the land. Down-hill master kangaroo has it all his own way. The bounds he takes are prodigious, and the fleetest hound is soon distanced. Up-hill the dogs have the best of it, and the run is a short one. It is when the chase lies over a plain that the best sport is seen. Then kangaroo and hounds are on equal footing, and the run is proportionally long and exciting.

There are many worse amusements than kangaroo hunting. Right pleasant is a gallop through the bush on a fine spring morning, when the earth is still fresh from recent rains, and Nature is at her freshest and greenest. With a bright sky above and the springy turf beneath— monarch of all he surveys, and at liberty to ride where and how he pleases, without having his ears dinned with cries of "Ware wheat!" "Ware turnips!"—or having his dander riz by seeing Farmer Giles and his retainers, pitchfork in hand, in battle arrayed to receive him, the kangaroo hunter can well dispense with the pomp and circumstance of an English hunting field.

Horsily attired as to his nether man, but saltish from the hips upwards—in Bedford cords, top-boots, flannel shirt, and cabbage-tree hat— half Jock half Jack—see him ride forth in the early morning. Mounted on his favourite steed, with his dogs behind him, he is as jolly as jolly can be. Like Sir Ralph the Rover—

> "He feels the cheering power of spring,
> It makes him whistle, it makes him sing."

But, unlike Sir Ralph, in his heart there is but little wickedness. His thoughts as he rides along are not of vengeance, pillage, and murder, but of his flocks and herds, of his little account with Messrs. Mortgage and Foreclose, his agents, of his balance at the Provincial Bank, of the day

he will most assuredly be found for sixteen hours
out of the twenty-four. He often remains there
for the night, sharing the hut and the tea,
mutton and damper, of the shepherds. Not only
is it a busy but an anxious time, for on the re-
sults of the lambing will depend the profits of the
current year. The wool going to pay station
expenses, it is from the increase that the squatter's profits are derived. Mr. Wight puts down
the minimum increase at 50 per cent. We
should much like to know on whose authority he
makes that statement. We are inclined to think
that he is his own authority, or that he has derived his information from the same individual
who told him that forty bushels of wheat to the
acre was an average yield. Instead of 50 per
cent. being the minimum, it would, under the
most favourable circumstances, be the maximum.
Supposing our friend Mr. Smith to have 20,000
sheep on his run, his yearly increase would, according to Mr. Wight, be 10,000. But out of
these 20,000 sheep, how many wethers and
maiden ewes are there? We do not, like him,
speak *ex cathedrá*, but we think we may venture
to say that it is an exceptional case where the
breeding ewes outnumber all the rams, wethers,
hoggets, and maiden ewes on the station.

Allowing that they formed one half of the entire number, for the yearly increase to reach Mr. Wight's minimum of 50 per cent. every one of them must have a lamb, every lamb dropped be weaned. But how many barren ewes are there in a flock! how many lambs dropped that are never weaned! In the year we visited Australia the lambing was a good one, yet, if we remember rightly, 80 per cent. was the estimated increase on the station where we passed the spring—80 per cent. on the entire number of ewes drafted for lambing. In every flock of 1000 ewes, 800 lambs were weaned and ear-marked. What proportion the breeders bore to the non-breeders we are unable to state. Allowing them to have been equally divided, the increase would have been at the rate of 40 per cent., or 10 per cent. less than Mr. Wight's minimum. Right happy would squatters be, we imagine, to accept Mr. Wight's minimum as their maximum, for at that rate any man beginning sheep-farming with a capital of 5000*l.* could return home at the end of ten years with a handsome competency. This would be a summary of his ten years' work, supposing that each year after shearing he culled and sold at four shillings a head one-fifth of the entire number :—

Years.		Sheep.		Increase.		Culls.
1	......	10,000	......	5,000	......	2,000
2	......	13,000	......	6,500	......	2,600
3	......	16,900	......	8,450	......	3,380
4	......	21,970	......	10,984	......	4,394
5	......	28,561	......	14,280	......	5,712
6	......	37,129	......	18,564	......	7,426
7	......	48,267	......	24,133	.....	9,653
8	......	62,747	......	31,373	......	12,549
9	......	81,571	......	40,765	......	16,314
10	......	106,642	......	53,021	......	

64,028

So that by the end of the tenth year he would
have 159,063 sheep, and have received in hard
cash for culls sold to butcher 12,806*l.* The
selling price of the station at ten shillings
per head would be 79,531*l.*—add 12,806*l.*, and
there is a grand total of 92,337*l.* Does the
reader think our calculation absurd? If he does,
let him cast an eye over the following table
showing the probable increase of an alpaca flock
as calculated by Mr. Wight:—

*" Table showing the probable increase of the alpaca flock. The
commencement is made with 200 females and 50 males.*

Females.	Lambs.	Females.	Males.					Males.	Females.	December.
200	120	60	60	at 60 ℔ cent. (allowing 10 per cent. for deaths)...				110	280	1861
200	120	60	60	,,	,,	Those dropt last year will not lamb		170	320	1862
280	160	80	80	,,	,,	The female lambs 1861 will drop this		250	400	1863
340	200	100	100	,,	,,	,,	1862 ,, ,,	350	500	1864
420	250	125	125	,,	,,	,,	1863 ,, ,,	475	625	1865
520	260	130	130	at 50 ℔ cent. only	,,	1864 ,, ,,		605	775	1866
645	520	160	160	,,	,,	,,	1865 ,, ,,	765	935	1867
775	387	190	190	,,	,,	,,	1866 ,, ,,	955	11	1868
935	467	235	235	,,	,,	,,	1867 ,, ,,	1195	1400	1869
1322	661	330	330	,,	,,	,,	1868 ,, ,,	1520	1730	1870

"There will be, after deduction made for wear and tear, accidents, &c., 3250, as per above calculation. We further deduct 25 per cent. of total every period of ten years, thus leaving in round numbers 2500; at the same rate, in

20 years there would be	.		20,000
30 ,, ,,	. . .		160,000
40 ,, ,,	. . .		1,280,000
50 ,, ,,	. . .		9,760,000

"At seven lbs. wool each—68,320,000 lbs., at 2s. per lb., 5,832,000l.!

"From this it will be seen that making deductions of a liberal nature, according to the present ratio of increase, there will be in fifty years 9,760,000 head, the wool of which, at 2s. per lb., will amount to the sum of 6,832,000l. per annum."

Such calculations cannot be otherwise than absurd, for, like the gambler's martingale, they are based upon the presumed recurrence of certain numbers or chances which may or may not turn up. A bad lambing throws the squatter back more than a year, for not only does he lose his profit, the lamb, but in losing the lamb the ewe which should in two or three years' time take the place of the cull sent to the pots or the butcher. And if a bad lambing season can upset the squatter's calculations, what shall be said of an excessively wet or of a dry one. However they may be ignored, such occurrences are not, we believe, altogether unknown in Australia. It strikes us that we have read somewhere or another of floods sweeping away flocks and herds wholesale, and of droughts, when sheep and cattle died by thousands for want of water. Nay, if we are not greatly mistaken, we have heard the words scab and foot-rot mentioned with a malediction by Australian squatters. Strange that when men sit down to calculate the probable gains they so invariably forget to leave a margin for the possible losses, and that they should always have such a vivid recollection of Messrs. Og and Gogg, who made their pile, and forget all about poor Jobus, who lost everything. That in an incredibly short space of time large fortunes have been made by sheep-farming we are perfectly aware, but we know likewise that fortunes have been lost in the same undertaking. Sheep-farming is undoubtedly one of the most profitable pursuits open to the gentleman emigrant of moderate capital, but to succeed there must be good management and good luck, and whatever may be said to the contrary, the latter is the more requisite of the two ; for whilst good luck will go far to counterbalance bad management, the best of management avails nothing against bad luck. Many a stupid has made his fortune—many a smart fellow has gone to the wall. One after another the different flocks lamb down, and before the last have ceased dropping shearing commences. Pens of sufficient size to hold an entire flock having been run up alongside the wash-pool, and booms laid across the creek or river on a level with the water in such a way as to prevent the sheep escaping when under manipulation, early one fine morning the first shepherd on the list drives his flock on to the ground, and the work of washing commences. On the appearance of the squatter, manager, or whoever may be the recognised boss of the wash-gang, the men take up their stations —one man in the main pen, two in the catching pen, two in the first water-pen or soak-hole, three in the second or washing ditto, two in the third or rinsing ditto, one in the fourth or exit. The signal being given, the man in the main pen drives a couple of hundred sheep or so into a smaller pen adjoining, some fifty of which he re-drafts into a third pen where the catchers are stationed. In an instant twenty sheep are swimming about in the soak-hole, whence they are passed by ducking their heads under the dividing boom to the men in the washing pen, who, after much rubbing and scrubbing, pass them in their turn to the men in the rinsing pen, who give them a finishing touch, after which they are allowed to make their escape to the shore, where the gentle shepherd is waiting to receive them. The washing over, the last sheep safely landed, Mr. Shepherd drives his flock to a clean camping-ground near the woolshed, in the pens attached to which building the said flock must be folded at an early hour in the morning, so that there may be no grumbling about having to wait on the part of the shearers.

Shortly after sunrise our squatter makes his appearance on the shearing-floor, and after entering the names of the shearers in his note-book, he gives the word to commence. Then twenty men make a dash at the catching pen; twenty sheep are lugged on to the floor, and twenty pair of shears commence clicking. All work their hardest, for not only is it every man's ambition to be boss-shearer of the crowd, but being paid by the score, the more sheep they shear the better the wages—the longer their "drunk" when the job is finished. As each fleece falls on the floor it is picked up by the hand told off for that purpose, who throws it on the sorting-table, where it is examined and rolled by the sorter ready for packing. When the last sheep in the catching-pen has been shorn, Mr. Squatter proceeds to call the roll, each shearer responding by shouting out the number of sheep he claims to have clipped, which number is entered against his name in the day-book. If the number actually shorn tally with the number given in by the shearers, a fresh lot are driven into the catching-pen, and the work proceeds as before. But if, as sometimes happens, the numbers do not tally, the work is suspended, each shearer is required to point out his sheep with their distinguishing ruddle mark, and in the event of any man not being able to do so he is fined for the delay his carelessness or greediness has occasioned. The rapidity with which some of these men whip off a fleece is surprising—five-score sheep a day being considered nothing extraordinary. But then the Australian Merino is smaller, and much lighter fleeced than the English Leicester or Southdown. As fast as the fleeces are rolled they are given to the man who presides at the screw-press to be packed, and, as fifteen hundred sheep are shorn daily, the bales of wool pile up quickly. Each bale is marked with Mr. Smith's initials and trade mark, H. E. S., with a W. W. in diamonds, and when there are a sufficient number of them to load two drays, the first instalment of the season's clip is despatched to the capital or nearest seaport. The last flock shorn, and the shearers departed, the yearly culling takes place. With his overseer as aid, Mr. Smith passes in final review all the sheep on the run, and drafts into one flock by themselves. for the pots such as he deems too old or too light-wooled or too coarse-wooled for profitable keeping.

With culling ends our squatter's year, and after giving instructions to his overseer respect-, ing the despatch of the wool, and the general management of the station during his absence, he starts for the capital.

His journey down is as uneventful as was his journey up, but before reaching the city he turns off the main road to visit the boiling-down esta-blishment of Hyde, Greaves, and Co., to make arrangements for the conversion of his culls into tallow. Our friend knows the road, but did he not do so he would only have to follow his nose to find it. At full half a mile distance from the works the air is tainted with the heavy smell of putrefying animal matter, the effluvium getting stronger as he advances, until the climax is reached at the door of the proprietor's cottage, which is built on an eminence overlooking the midden, where tons upon tons of carrion lie reek-ing in the sun. One gets used to everything; and Mr. Greaves has become so habituated to the deadly stench that he hardly perceives it. Indeed, from the touchy way in which he resents any allusion to stinks and stenches, one would be almost inclined to think that he enjoyed it.

Mr. Smith's arrangements are soon made. For one shilling a head his sheep are to be boiled down, and the pelts and tallow delivered free of charge to his agents. Supposing them to average fifteen pounds of tallow, four shillings a head clear of expenses is what he may expect to receive for them—not one-third of what they would be worth "tinned" for European consumption. But until the meatless million can overcome their stupid prejudices, or rather, perhaps, until the Australian meat preserver can supply his beef and mutton at a lower price than he does at present, the squatter's fat sheep must go the pots, and the meat be thrown on the dung-heap. Considering the present price of stock in Australia, sevenpence a pound appears to us a ridiculously high figure. When it comes down to fivepence, a good deal of the present prejudice against it will vanish, and boiling-down establishments cease to be numbered amongst Australian institutions.

Settling day has come at last, and as the clock strikes ten, Mr. Smith, with his cheque-book in his breast-pocket, and his account-

books under his arm, walks into the office of
Messrs. Mortgage and Foreclose, his agents.
It is not every squatter who is able to mark the
day with a white stone. When Mr. Squatter
is heavily indebted to his agents, and the year's
clip and lambing have been unsatisfactory, it
is a very black day indeed. His little calculations not having come off, instead of the
balance being in his favour it is all the other
way, and not only is he unable to pay off any
portion of the debt, but even to meet the interest. His agents, although exceedingly obliging
fellows in some respects, are very Shylocks in
enforcing the punctual repayment of their
moneys. They hold a lien on his flocks and
herds, and he knows that unless they consent to
give him time he is a gone squatter. Even
should they agree to do so, he is very far from
being out of the toils, for he will have to pay
heavily for the accommodation, not only in the
shape of compound interest, but in that of "incidental expenses," which, however unjust, tax
he dare not. No wonder that he leaves the
counting-house with a long face and a heavy
heart. What a fool he has been! Why, when
counting up the probable gains, did he so
stupidly forget to leave a margin for the losses ?
If he had for a moment imagined that this, that,

and the other would have happened, he would never have borrowed money. That's just it. If the squatter could only know beforehand how things would turn out, there would be no risk in borrowing money at a high rate of interest. As he cannot, the risk he runs is considerable. Mr. Smith having purchased his station, cash down, has the whip hand of his agents. He is not afraid to tax their account, or to point out an overcharge or "clerical error." If they don't strike out this, deduct that, let the account be closed—he will find other agents. The threat is sufficient. The firm of F. M. & Co. are always ready to do what's fair. Sooner than have any unpleasantness the pen shall go through the item in dispute. Mr. Smith they are ready to oblige; they would see Mr. Hardup hanged first. By the time the last entry in the account-book has been audited, the list of deductions to be made is a long one; but when it has been totted up, and the sum total subtracted, Mr. Smith expresses himself satisfied, shakes hands with the partners, and takes his departure. Every reason has he to be satisfied. If the increase of his flocks has not been fifty per cent., it has been little short of forty. Although he has not suc-ceeded in making a shilling a head pay the working expenses of his station, the money received for the clip will more than cover them, and there will be a few hundred pounds coming in for tallow. Lastly, Messrs. Mortgage and Foreclose have not got the better of him to the value of one shilling, and that is a cause for jubilation. His first year at Waddy-Waddy has been a good one, and after his twelve months' work he has earned his little holiday. Let us hope that he enjoys it, and that after a few years he will have amassed sufficient to enable him to return to that best of all good countries—OLD ENGLAND.

THE END.

www.ingramcontent.com/pod-product-compliance
Lightning Source LLC
Chambersburg PA
CBHW020859020726
47497CB00005B/1473